COMFORT IN PAIN

Lola Grant

Contents

Pleasure

Olivia's POV

My mother always used the excuse, "I brought you into this world and I can take you out," the only difference with my mother saying it and other mothers saying it is that mine actually meant it. I mean like, I never asked to be born. If you want to take me out please do it and quickly. The faster I can leave this shit hole the better.

Maybe it's because she never wanted me, which is understandable. I'm a lot to deal with. I have a lot of issues. But to be fair, every single one of those issues were because of her and my father. Honestly, they weren't even my parents. They were just the people who had me. I think I would have done better in the foster care system.

And that's saying a lot.

People always tell me that I should be thankful that I have parents and that my father stuck around after my mother had me instead of 'going to get the milk'. But in reality, I would have been so fucking happy if he went to go get the milk. I would have been mentally stable if my mother left me at the doorstep of a fire station.

Every time I have these thoughts I hate myself for it. I hate that I blame my mother for what happened. Something terrible happened to her and as a result, she had me and was stuck with my father. Now him on the other hand, I resented him. He was the reason for my trauma, he was the reason why I am the way I am.

But he never hit me. He never raised his voice at me. He never touched me. He never did anything. And yet I hate him. I hate him because of what he did to my mother. My mother has hit me, my mother has always raised her voice at me, honestly, I don't even know what her regular voice sounds like, but I don't hate her.

I sighed frustratedly as I laid there in my bed. Three months ago I finally moved out of my parents house, and out of the state. A New Yorker in Virginia. Wasn't that big of a difference but there are a lot less people. I was also more happy here. Don't get me wrong, I still had my days where my past haunted me, but for the most part I was fine. I work, go to school, and have enough money to not make me a broke college student. I looked to my right at my clock to see I had about twenty minutes to get to my first class.

It takes me twenty-five minutes to get there.I sighed as I got out of bed and got dressed. I'm studying to be a photographer, which at this point I think I should change career paths. Photography just seemed like an easy job and I do like taking pictures, but why the fuck do I have to take a fucking math class. Which by the way, not the best way to start your day.

Within fifteen minutes I was at school and the bell had just rung. I groaned as I walked into my class. The door shut loudly behind me causing everyone to look at me. My teacher, Mrs. Moore, gave me a glare. As a child growing up in a terrible household, I learned to mask my anger and sadness and literally every fucking feeling with humor. So I just smiled at her and went to go find my seat.

I sat down by my friend and she just rolled her eyes at me. "Are you ever on time?" She whispered. I shrugged my shoulders and took out my notebook.

'"Why the fuck did any of us sign up for a class this early?" I said back. I'm surprised I haven't dropped this class.

Oh wait, I haven't because Mrs. Moore is hot.

The rest of the class I was stuck in my own head. Whatever that woman was rambling on about, I knew Pagie would write it down and give it to me later. I felt her tap my shoulder and I looked at her. "You okay? You seem off," I just slightly smiled and nodded my head. I knew she knew I was lying but still.

Class ended soon enough and I stretched hard as I laid down on the bench outside the classroom. Paige looked down at me with a look of concern I couldn't help but menallty laugh. Paige and I have been friends for about three months now. Every friend I've ever made only lasted for the school year so I never really put in effort to make friends. Paige seems different though. She acts as if she really cares about me which is a foreign feeling to me. So instead of embracing it, I push her away.

I watched as she wrote down something and handed it to me. I looked to see a number. "I already have your number stupid. And this isn't even your number," she rolled her eyes and I laughed.

"That's the number of a therapist I've heard of," this time it was my turn to roll my eyes. I stood up and started walking towards the cafeteria. Paige followed and slapped my shoulder. She has a problem with hitting people. "I'm serious. I've heard she's really good at what she does-"

"Paige, all therapist are useless. They just steal quotes from books and say it to you. Then make you pay $150 for every damn quote. Thank you but pass," Paige stood in front of me and stopped me.

"Look, I know we haven't known each other for very long but I care about you. And clearly you have had something very traumatic happen to you. Now, I hope some day we will get to the point where you can tell me but right now, I can see we're not there. So I am giving you this because I want you to talk to someone," I looked at the red head in front of me, curiously.

Why is it always the red heads that are most companionate?

I took her hand in mine and squeezed it, giving her a sincere look. "Thank you. But the things I've went through is something I can handle on my own," I watched as defeat settled in her eyes and she nodded her head. We continued to walk to the cafeteria in silence.

All in while I shoved the number in my back pocket.

****

I only have two classes for today, thankfully. So about time I got home I was too awake to go back to sleep. I looked around my apartment and bit my bottom lip. I moved in here at the beginning of the year and I have yet to decorate. It's my final year in college and honestly I don't know what the hell I'm going to do with my life.

After high school in New York I wanted to move for college but I couldn't. As much as I hated it my mother was right. I wasn't ready to move. I didn't know much about the outside world. I didn't understand bills or taxes. I always felt that when I turned into an adult I would be put in jail for something I didn't do. Like my taxes. And the reason for that would be because I didn't know how to do that shit.

So I stayed in New York for three more years for college. Then once I finished my junior year I couldn't take it anymore so I moved.

I reached into my back pocket and felt the little piece of paper. I argued with myself on if I should do it or not. I always assumed no one cared about me so I never talked about my problems, I just kept them to myself.

I looked at the paper to see a number and a name. Dr. Morgan. V.M I chuckled seeing as they had a first last name. I groaned as I pulled out my phone and dialed the number. "Hello?" A voice said. All of a sudden I felt like I was making a dentist appointment and started stuttering.

"Um h-hi. Is Dr. Morgan available?" The voice on the other end went quiet and I mentally slapped myself in the face. What the hell am I doing? I was about to hang up then the voice came again.

"She just got done with a patient. If you are near she can squeeze you in now," this time I went silent. I wasn't expecting to fucking see her today! "If not, you have to wait to next week," I swallowed the lump in the back of my throat.

"Ugh yeah, I'm on my way,"

"What's your name sweetheart?" I guess I clearly sound like a child.

"Olivia, Olivia Miller,"

"Great, I will see you soon Ms. Olivia," I hung up the phone and I started feeling my nerves slowly creep in.

I walked to my bathroom and took three of my anti-anxiety pills. This crap doesn't work for shit. I left my apartment, locking the door behind me. I typed in the address into Google maps and within 10 minutes I was standing in front of a tall white building.

The building just screamed Therapist. V. M was plastered across the top of the building. I took one final breath and walked in.

Immediately I was filled with the smell of Vanilla. Not going to lie, I felt something inside of me lighten. How can a place or a smell change your mood? I never understood that.

I walked up to the lady behind a desk and told her my name. She told me to ride the elevator to the top floor and so I obeyed.

The elevator played calm music as if it was trying to seduce you. And if I'm being honest, it was working.

The doors opened and I was shocked. The entire downstairs including the outside of the building and the elevator was covered in white.

But this floor was red. As red as a rose.

It took me a second to step forward because I was too amazed with my surroundings. "Ms. Olivia?" I turned my head to the simi-familiar voice. There was a smiling woman standing besides me. She held out her hand and I hesitantly shook it. "It's nice to meet you. I'm Violet,"

I smiled at the woman and my nerves started to slightly slow down. "Nice to meet you," I let go of her hand and she directed me to a room.

"Ms. Morgan is waiting for you," I got confused a bit until I realized that she wasn't the therapist. I got a little sad seeing as she seemed welcoming. She nodded her head towards the door and walked away back to her desk.

I looked at the door as if my worst nightmare was behind the damn thing and finally opened the door.

The room seemed simple yet elegant. Quiet, but loud, welcoming. But also not. For a therapist this woman is confusing. "Have a seat Ms. Miller," my heart jumped a little as the voice came. I looked up to see a woman searching through a draw.

I didn't pay much attention to her because I didn't plan on staying.

I sat down in the red chair and put my hands between my legs. The sound of heels clicked against the tile floor and soon the woman came into my full view.

I felt the lump in the back of my throat come back and my mouth became dry. She sat down in front of me and crossed her legs. Her grey eyes stared deep into mine as if she was just waiting for me to stutter. "I'm Dr. Morgan, and it's a pleasure to meet you,"

Dr. Morgan

Three years ago, I realized I was a lesbian. I know, kind of off topic but I just felt the need the bring that up. I've never slept with anyone, had sex, done anything remotely close to it. I don't know why but I've never had the urge to do so. No one has ever made me want them in a sexual manner.

I mean of course I've masterbated, who the hell hasn't. But no one has ever made me horny. Like ever.

And looking back at it, I think the main reason for that was because I was looking in the wrong direction. The day I finally took a step out of my comfort zone, was the day I realized no one ever made me horny because I was only looking at men.

Women.

That's a whole nother story.

So you best believe when I tell you, as I was sitting in front of this woman who looked like she wanted to tear me down from the inside and out, my insides were burning.

I was conflicted between being intimidated, the way her eyes pierced into mine, the way her legs were crossed over one another, the way she was leaning back with a notepad in her lap, she had on a pencil skirt and a white blouse. Her chest was slightly showing and my pervert ass couldn't take my eyes off them.

My hands were still between my legs and I could feel them starting to sweat. I've never done therapy nor shared my feelings so I don't know if this intense staring in supposed to happen or not.

Why the fuck am I still here?

I cleared my throat and looked everywhere but at her. I could feel her still staring at me and it felt like the side of my head was burning. "Nice place you have," I said, finally breaking the silence.

I did the unthinkable and looked at her. She was wearing glasses which just made things worse.

The things I was feeling were unnatural for me. I kept shifting in my chair, I started scratching my arm as I do when I'm nervous, and couldn't stop biting my bottom lip. "Thank you,"

A vibration went straight through my body as the words left her mouth. I looked up at her to see her still looking at me. But the look in her eyes were now filled with a hint of amusement. "What, exactly, am I supposed to talk about?" I asked. She squinted her eyes at me as if she was trying to figure something out, which is understandable considering she's a therapist, but what wasn't understandable was the look that meant she already knew who I was.

"Whatever your comfortable with," I slightly scoffed and put my hand to the side of my head.

"If that's the case, I would walk out the door," I watched as she slowly nodded her head and wrote something down. What the fuck is she writing?!

Ha, when you make a joke with your therapist, and instead of them laughing they write something down.

"You know yourself and you know what your comfortable sharing, so share that,"

"But what if I don't know myself,"

"Figure it out," the room went silent as we looked at one another. Anger rose in body but the way she was staring at me had me scared to move. I cleared my thoughts and scoffed.

"Why am I even here," I stood up and walked towards the door.

"You get offended very easily,"

"I dont get offended easily, I just don't like wasting my fucking time on someone who just wants my money," I watched as the woman watched me, she hasn't moved from that position since she sat down.

My eyes slowly dropped to her legs. She looks good in what she's wearing but she seems like a suit type woman. I swallowed the lump in my throat as I realized she was still watching me. "Five minutes," I squinted my eyes at her. "You lasted for five minutes before you wanted to leave. Sweatheart, even I can last longer than that,"

"And how long exactly can you last,"

"Longer than your tiny ass could handle," she said that just above a whisper as her eyes scanned my body. I felt another vibration run through me and I couldn't handle it. I just shook my head and opened the door. "Your parents treated you like shit," I paused. Silence followed and I knew she wasn't going to finsih until I turned around, so I did. "But you only hated one. You hate yourself for being born. You don't make friends because you think they're going to leave you," she tilted her head to the side and grinned. "And you have serious mommy issues," I put my shoulders back, trying to look intimidating but her stare was making it hard.

"And what makes you think that?" She rose her head a little, and that simple move had more confidence in it than my entire person.

"Because you haven't been able to keep your eyes off me since you got in here,"

"Well you're a very beautiful woman, no doubt men can't keep they're eyes off you," she was getting ready to say something back but instead she just gestured with her hand for me to sit.

I sighed seeing as she has gotten her facts right. So far.

"I think that's enough talking from me," she said as I closed the door and sat back down in the seat. "Now it's your turn," I leaned back in the chair and threw my head back. There was no point in trying to impress this woman seeing as I'll never be seeing her again.

"Ugh, I'm in college, I just moved here not too long ago, I want to murder everyone around me except my one friend. She's probably going to end up leaving me anyways," it was quiet for a minute so I moved my head to see her staring at my neck. I started rubbing it, checking if I had some type of scar on.

"And why do you say that?" I shrugged my shoulders and slightly chuckled. I tilted my head to the side and squinted my eyes at her. Do people really do this for a living? Ask people questions about their lives, pretending that they're actually helping them?

"If you already know the answer, what's the point in asking?" She didn't say anything but stared. I don't know this woman but she's already starting to annoy me.

"I wanna hear you say it,"

"Say what?" She uncrossed her legs and leaned forward.

"Something terrible happened to you and you won't be able to move past it unless you stop running running from it and face it," deep down I knew she was right but I would never admit it. No doubt she could see the anger and annoyance inside my eyes so she just leaned back. "How old are you Ms. Miller?"

"21," she nodded and wrote it down. I watched as she stood up to see she is much taller than I thought.

"What about you? How old are you?" She looked down at me, no doubt I looked like an ant she can step on with those damn heels.

"Too old for you if that's what your thinking?" I threw my hands up and shook my head as she walked towards her desk.

"Eh, no disrespect. But I am curious. Is it Ms. or Mrs.-" I paused seeing as I don't know her first name. She looked up at me from shuffling through papers.

"It's Dr." I nodded in respect and stood up.

"Well, nice to know, because if I ever-"

"I would watch your mouth if I were you," my knees became a little weak making me grab on to the chair. I don't know what it is, but the way her voice flows from my ears through my body paralyzes me.

"Or what?"

She put down the papers in her hand and slowly walked around her desk and towards me. I did my best not to back away but my instincts took over me and I took one step back which was enough to have my ass hit the couch.

She stopped when she was in front of me and leaned forward to where I could smell the lavender scent roaming off her.

"Don't tempt me,"

Drunk Call

The sound of a fly buzzing around my head had me going crazy. My first thought was that I died and turned into spiderman, now I can hear things up close. But when I opened my eyes, I was sadly disappointed to find out I wasn't spiderman, and that I indeed that the biggest fucking headache.

The smallest movement on the bed caused it to squeak loudly making me groan in pain. Another groan from across the room came and I sighed of relief a bit seeing as Paige was with me.

I looked around to see we were in her room. I don't remember how we got here, nor do I recall when we got here. I looked down to see I was still in my clothes from last night.

I tried to move my legs but the leather prevented me from doing so. I gave up at some point and just laid back down. "What time is it?" Paige asked while whining.

"Does it matter? There's no way in hell either of us is getting up, never the less, going to class," I responded. The last thing I remember was some guy buying me a drink while attempting to flirt with me.

The bartender watched him the entire time and gave me an 'okay' nod, letting me know the guy didn't strike it with something.

"What the hell happened?" Paige asked as she slowly got off the floor and flopped on to the bed.

"Your asking the wrong person," I grabbed my phone off the night stand and opened it. It was nearly noon and I just sighed.

"Rule one of a hangover," Paige said as she grabbed her phone. "Check to make sure you didn't make a drunk call to anyone," I snorted and slightly laughed as I went to my call logs.

It took a second for my brain to process the number, but once I did, I damn near threw up. I apparently stayed on the phone for three minutes saying God knows what.

I rolled off the bed and grabbed the first pair of shoes I saw. Unfortunately, they were the heels I wore last night. "What's the matter?" I started whine seeing as I don't know what the hell I said.

"I called your fucking therapist office last night! I don't know what the fuck I said, but seeing as I say dumb shit when I'm drunk, probably nothing good!" Paige started laughing as she rolled on her back and watched me struggle.

I quickly looked at myself in her mirror and mentally slapped myself. "Have fun explaining yourself!" Paige yelled after me as I rushed out her house. I fucking hate her.

I hailed a cab and the way he was looking at me and out of breath I was, it looked like I was fleeing from a one night stand. He drove me to the building and I quickly got out and paid him.

I went inside and speed walked to the elevator.

I know I've already been here, but the color change from the building to this floor always catches me off guard. I walked out the elevator and the receptionist, Violet, looked up at me. Her eyes scanned my body and she forced a smile. "Ms. Olivia. I didn't expect you back so soon,"

"Me neither. Is she here?" I asked pointing to Dr. Morgan's office.

"Yes, but-" I didn't even let her finished and opened the door. There was a woman sitting in the same seat I sat last time with her head in her hands. Both of them looked up at and if it wasn't for the fear I was feeling from calling her office I would have felt humiliated right now. But the fear clouded that humiliation.

"Miss Miller. I know your young but I would assume you have the basic human skills to not interpret me when I with-"

"Yes, I'm so so sorry. But I really need to talk to you. Right now." The woman looked between me and Dr. Morgan and stood up and grabbed her purse.

"I'll see you next week dr." she walked past me and I kind of felt bad.

I went into the room and closed the door behind me. When I turned around Dr. Morgan was staring at me. I was about to say something but the look she was giving me told me to shut up. I cleared my throat and put my hands together. "If you're going to barge in here as if I owe you something, I expect you to be making demands not standing there looking like some clueless imp," my insides started to turn as I looked down at my feet.

"I-I'm sorry. I just n-need to talk...ask you something,"

"Then ask it," she was still sitting down in her seat and was still glaring at me. I took a deep breath and went to go sit down on the couch.

"I went out with a friend last night,"

"I see that," She whispered as she looked over my clothes. "Leather. That's a woman's game," she cocked her head to the side. "Are you a woman Miss Miller?" I swallowed the lump in the back of my throat as we stared at one another. The room was silent, her green eyes pierced through mine. I watched as she shifted in her seat and uncrossed her legs.

"I called your office last night. I was drunk and I don't know why, of all the numbers on my phone, I called your office. But I would like to apologize for anything misleading or inappropriate I might have said," never did she once take her eyes off me. I started moving around in my seat, feeling uncomfortable under her stare.

"I take my work very seriously. I help people with their problems. I take the scared, helpless little person inside them, and I strike it down. I make them new. I make them confident. I make it to where no one tells them what to do. No one controls their life but them," she leaned forward. "And no one, tells them no," I watched as a grin appeared on her face sending shivers down my spine. "I turn them into me," I watched as she stood up while still looking at me.

She hovered over me and my face was in line with her abdomen. My eyes started from her jet black hair that was in a bun, to her eyes that just seem to see right through me. Her chest that made her blouse look like a t-shirt, her stomach that I wanted to run my lips over so bad, to her legs, causing me to bite my bottom lip. Something caught my attention though before I looked back at her.

Something was poking out of her skirt.

Once she noticed I was staring, she walked away from me and went to her desk. I let out a deep breath that I didn't even know I was holding in. I stood up and made my way towards the door. "One more thing Miss Miller," I turned around to look at her. She was sitting down typing something on her computer with a smirk on her face. "I would watch who call when your drunk. Not that I minded what I heard,"

Leather

I walked into school with my bag basically pulling me down to the ground. I don't even know what's in this fucking thing. All I know is that I want to throw all these damn books at my professors. "Olivia!" I turned around, tiredly, to see Paige rushing towards me.

I didn't get much sleep last night because the thought of Dr. Morgan stayed in my head. There's something about that woman that just allures me to her. And seeing as I've only seen her once and I can't keep my mind off her, it's pissing me off.

"Wassup?" I said as I yawned. Paige squinted her eyes at me as if yawning and being tired isn't normal. "Before you say anything, I went to your therapist," I watched as a smile started to creep onto her face. I held up my hand. "Don't get excited, I'm not going back,"

"Why?!" I slightly chuckled and started walking away. She followed behind like a lost puppy, pouting.

"Because it wasn't any more helpful than me just talking to myself. And at least that's free," I had given the receptionist my card number and crap after I left. I know I could have just walked out without paying because I know I'll never see them again, but I'm just not that type of person. But surprisingly, my card hasn't been charged yet. I'm going to give them to the end of the day to charge my card, otherwise, I'm just going to pay my rent with it.

Ugh. Adulthood.

"But did you like it? Did she know what she was talking about? Did she act weird?" I stopped walking and turned to look at her.

"What do you mean, 'weird'?" she nervously smiled and walked past me into our class. The bell rang above our heads as we found our seats. "Don't act like you can just ignore me," I said. Mrs. Moore walked in looking hot as always causing me to forget about Paige for a second.

"Pick up your mouth before you start drooling," Paige whispered. I rolled my eyes at her and grabbed her hand. "Why would the therapist act weird?" Paige sighed and looked at the front of the class to make sure Mrs. Moore wasn't listening.

"The people I know that have gone to her say she's weird," I leaned back surprised, very tempted to scream.

"Why the hell would you send me to someone who's fucking crazy?!" I whisper yelled.

"So she does act weird? My bad," she slightly laughed and I couldn't help but roll my eyes at her.

"Alright, class. Take out your notes from yesterday. Pop quiz," literally everyone in class groaned making Mrs. Moore chuckle. I'm not saying that I haven't been paying attention, but let's just say, I'm not going to pass this damn quiz.

She handed out the papers and the people in the front handed them back. I looked at the questions and it hit me. The only thing I knew was my name and the date. Hell, I didn't even know the date. I looked over at Paige to see her already on question three.

After about five minutes I just started circling random things. At some point, I circled C four times in a row and knew one of them was wrong.

We handed back our papers and at this point, I was just ready to leave. "But in all seriousness, how did it go?" I sighed as I leaned back. I crossed my arms and stared at Mrs. Moore as she collected the papers.

"It wasn't that bad. But like I said, not going back," Paige wrapped her arm around me and leaned her head on my shoulder.

"You are so damaged," I chuckled and nodded my head.

The day went on playfully slow with a certain long-legged lady on my mind. Paige was walking me home and must have noticed I was zoned out. "You good?" I nodded my head and tripped over air making her laugh.

"Ok, this Dr. Morgan, what can you tell me about her?" Paige shrugged her shoulders making me want to choke the shit out of her. "Fine, can you at least tell me her first name?" Once I saw her struggling with that I stopped walking and threw my arms. "What the fuck! You sent me to some woman whose name you don't even know?" Paige slowly started to smile.

"My bad," I put my hand to my forehead annoyed. Her laughing wasn't helping at all. Whatever, it doesn't matter. I'm not going back anyway so there's no point in questioning Paige or in my case, yelling at her.

We started back walking with some small talk here and there, and honestly, I wished it stayed that way. "So, we going out tonight right?"

"You know, in every kidnapped, murder-themed type movie, it always starts with the best friend saying "let's go out"," she playfully punched me in the shoulder making me smile. I haven't gone out in ages. If I really think about it, I don't think I've actually ever "gone out" before. I'm more of a book worm and that's how I like it. I love the way you get lost in the world you're making in your head with the words your reading.

It's even better when your writing. Because in that way, you're creating that world, you're making those characters come to life. And your making other people fall in love with those characters that you personally made.

I must have been zoned out for a minute because Paige was snapping her fingers in front of my face and we were standing in front of my building. "There's no point in arguing with me because I will drag you if I have to," I groaned while rolling my eyes and walked away. "Be ready by 10, and wear something leather!" I flicked her off and walked into the building.

Who the fuck wears leather? Other than a leather jacket. I don't see how people do it. Leather pants seem cute on certain people but I'm not one of those people. How do you even put them on?!

I started mentally punching Paige because she had me thinking about leather now.

******

About time 10 rolled around I was very tempted to fall onto my bed and go to sleep. I wouldn't have agreed to go seeing as it's the middle of the damn week, but I don't have class till eleven so I should be good. I don't plan on staying out long. Just long enough to get Paige off my back.

I did the unthinkable and actually wore leather. Just the jacket though.

A knock rang through my apartment and I went to open the door. Paige stood in front of me with a wide smile and a bottle in her hand. I rolled my eyes and let her in. "Put this on and let's go," she threw some pants at me and I looked at them to see they were leather.

"Imma needs a minute," I said looking over them. They were pretty cute I'll give her that.

Ten minutes later I finally had them on. I tucked in a black shirt and put on my 'too nice to wear out' heels. I looked myself over and decided I will stay out longer. This outfit is too nice not to be shown. I walked out of my room and Immediately Paige started cat-calling me. Redheads are so innocent to the eye but so dirty once you get to know them. "Let's go you whore," I said as I grabbed my purse.

"I would rather be a whore than a 21-year-old virgin," my mouth gaped open wide as she walked past me with a smirk. We left the apartment and made our way downstairs. "Why do we never take the elevator?"

"Because I would rather not die by an elevator then an hour later the police find me wearing this and assume I was a hooker," Paige snorted.

"I'm pretty sure once they do the autopsy they will look up your vagina and see how tight you are and rule out you weren't a hooker. And you died a virgin,"

"oh my fucking god!" I yelled making her laugh.

We got into her car and made our way to this club that was somewhat out of town. As soon as I stepped out of the car, the smell of alcohol and sex filled my nose. This seemed to arouse Paige as she smiled and closed the car door. "Let's go get you laid mamas," I rolled my eyes and sighed deeply.

We walked into the club and music immediately took over my ears. I looked around at the people to see them all dancing or drinking, or sticking each other's tounges down one another's throats. As I looked around more I felt a certain pair of eyes on me.

Name

I sat there in my class on my computer. It's my last class of the day and I'm already done with everything. The room is pretty quiet right now and that's the only reason why I'm staying here instead of going home. A quiet room with people is better than a quiet room by myself. Cause if I hear something I would know it's someone else, rather than if I was by myself, then Megalodon could be swimming in my toilet.

I was sitting in the back by myself scrolling through Google. There is a slight...high possibility I'm looking up Dr. Morgan right now.

I was surprised to see there was a lot of information that came up about her. There were pictures of her, all with her wearing her hair in a bun. Apparently, she's 37. She was born in Virginia. And founder and owner of V.M.

The only thing I didn't find was her first name. Since she owns that damn building, I'm assuming it starts with a V. How the hell does Google know how old she is but doesn't know her name?

Dr. Morgan is an amazing, beautiful, talented woman. She got me through my divorce, helped me find myself, and helped me become a strong independent woman. She has many different techniques, some were very helpful and I couldn't thank her enough. -Avery Allen

I read through dozens of different reviews, and all of them just said how wonderful she was. No one mentioned her first name at all only making my curiosity stronger. There was one review though that caught my attention.

This woman should have her license taken away! She should not professionally nor legally be able to have patients. She should be in jail, not in a position where she holds power over people! She is a sexual predator and should be stopped! She isn't normal. She's not a true woman! -Anonymous

54 people liked the comment and I couldn't stop reading it over and over again. Especially the last sentence. If she isn't a "true woman" then why do they keep refering to her as a she? I sighed as I clicked out of the reviews and went back to the pictures of her.

My eyes couldn't help but roam to how perfect her lips were. Not too small, not too big, they were just perfect. I started to daydream about my lips on hers. I started biting my lower lip and slightly rocking my hips against my chair.

The look in her eyes held power as they always do. She had her glasses off, she was wearing a black blazer and pants that flowed a little at the bottom.

I felt something between my legs starting to throb. My breathing quickened as I kept rocking my hips. I felt wetness starting to form in my underwear. I kept looking at the picture and the way she was looking at me damn near had me on my knees. I closed my eyes and covered my mouth as "Are you okay?" I jumped up and opened my eyes. I looked up to see Mrs. Moore squinting at me. I cleared my throat and crossed my legs.

"Y-Yeah I'm fine. Just trying to think how I'm going to change my work hours," she nodded her head slowly as if she knew I was lying.

I have Mrs. Moore for three classes and this is the only one I have with her by myself. "Looking up Dr. Morgan, huh?" I turned to my computer and sighed.

"Yeah. I'm doing a research paper and she seemed like an interesting person," Mrs. Moore bit her lip and crossed her arms. "What? You don't agree with me?" I asked with a hint of amusement in my voice. She slightly smiled and shook her head.

"No, I just," she sighed deeply. "I've met her before. And ugh, to make it easier on you, I would suggest you research someone else. There's nothing special about that woman. She's closed off, she keeps to herself and as you can tell, no one knows her first damn name. Except probably her contractor," I mentally agreed with her.

"Well thank you," I looked up at her and leaned back in my seat, and smirked. "You're looking very stunning today, Angela," she rolled her eyes at me and I quietly chuckled.

Mrs. Moore and I have had a little flirting here and there. Nothing harmful though because I know she is married. We've only known each other for a few months but we've gotten close. When I first moved here, Angela was the first professor I made friends with. We built a simi-friendship, where I flirt with her and she kicks me out of class.

"Shut the hell up," I chuckled as she walked away back to her desk. I leaned back in my seat as I side looked at the picture again. I closed my computer shut rolling my eyes at myself.

It's been a week since I've last seen her and it's like she's mentally taunting me. This woman is apparently so known in this town, and yet, I've never heard of her up until two weeks ago.

I decided that torturing myself with these thoughts and questions with no answers was useless and that I should go get some answers. I packed up my things and walked down the stairs to the front of the room. "Olivia," I turned my head to see Angela motioning to come to her. I walked to her and smiled. She snorted and leaned forward. "My husband is out of town and I'm bored," If I wasn't a virgin and scared to lose it, I would have screwed this woman the moment I laid eyes on her. Before I knew she was married.

"Is this a booty call?" She put her hand over her forehead making me slightly laugh.

"No. I just wanted to see if you wanted to go do something later tonight," I smiled to myself.

"Last time I went out it didn't end so well,"

"Well, there isn't going to be any drinking," I squinted my eyes at her and she just smiled. "I'm pregnant," my mouth opened wide and I quietly squealed. I put down my bag and hugged her tightly. "Get the hell off me," I chuckled and moved back.

"In that case, I will be more than happy to go do something with you tonight," I put up my finger. "Can you not drink the entire pregnancy, or can you drink within the first few months?"

"Bye Olivia," I laughed while picking up my bag and walked out of the classroom.

I hailed a cab and he drove me to the building. I went inside and up the elevator to her floor and I couldn't help but stop and stare. There's something about the red decor that just captures your attention. I walked up to her door but before I opened it I stopped. I looked to my right to surprisingly not seeing Violet.

I knocked on the door and stepped back. The door opened a minute later and Violet stepped out while fixing her hair. Dr. Morgan was right behind her and they both looked up and saw me. I slightly smirked while looking away. A touch of jealousy lingered in the back of my head but I ignored it. "Ms. Wilson, I wasn't expecting you," I sarcastically smiled.

"Me neither, but I just keep coming back. So I thought I might as well make my time here worth while," I said while looking at her. i turned my head to look at Violet and a cocky smile glazed her lips.

"I guess I don't see the harm," Violet sharply turned her head to Dr. Morgan as if saying 'what the hell'. I didn't bother on staying for the glaring contest so I walked into her office and sat down. They continued to talk for a minute or so then the door closed. I crossed my legs and put my fist under my chin and looked up at her. "So, to what do I owe the pleasure of this visit?"

"Well, you are my therapist," She chuckled and nodded her head as she went to go sit down in her seat.

"In that case, I think we need to make it offcial," I titled my head up in questioning as she sat down. "I need to start charging you," I smiled while nodding and turned my head and pulled my hair into a ponytail. She watched me the entire time, something in her eyes changed but I couldn't pin point it. "So, whats been going on with you lately," I leaned my head on my fist and looked at the woman in front of me.

She was everything and nothing like the woman in the picture.

"Is there a problem Ms. Wilson?" she said straight forward. I leaned back in my seat with my legs still crossed. This seemed to impress her.

"You are very well known Dr. Morgan," the side of her lips curled into a grin. "Everyone seems to love you. They say that they learned from you. That you changed their life drastically. They praise you," I tilted my head again, which is what I do when I'm trying to read someone. Which is probably useless seeing that reading people is her job. "Your a very devious woman Dr. Morgan,"

"I prefer the term strategic thinker,"

I closed my eyes for a second and slightly smiled. "But others. They seem to think that you don't deserve what you have. What you do. That you're closed off. That you keep to yourself. That you're not intresting,"

That grin stayed on her face the entire time. "You looked me up," I didn't respond but instead stared at her. She bit her bottom lip. "Am I allowed to ask who said those things about me?" I continued to stare at her. Her grin turned into a smile and she looked up at the ceiling. "Fine," she looked back at me. "Is there a question here?"

I uncrossed my legs and leaned forward. "After everything that I found about you, and what I've heared, and what I've seen, there was only one question that lingered," she rose her head in quetioning. "What's your name?" The room went silent. This seemed to not be what she thought I was going to ask, so she laughed. "Fine, if you won't tell me, then I'll just come up with one for you. Because calling you Dr. Morgan in my head is getting tiring" she leaned back in her seat and put her finger to her lips.

"So you think about me a lot then?" A cocky smile formed. "My assistant doesn't even know my first name. And we're very close in some aspects. Or at least she thinks so," The look in my eyes held indifference, even though I know what she just said will be on my mind all night. "But hey, be my guest," I looked over her. All her features, aspects, components. I even tried to read her aura.

"Your real name starts with V, so." I tapped my finger against my chin. "Venessa," she rose her eyebrow. "Venessa Morgan. I like the sound of that," she chuckled and stood up.

"Then Venessa it is," she said in a deep tone sending shivers finger my spine. She walked over to her bookshelf.

"Your really not going to tell me your name?" her back was facing to me, and my eyes couldn't help but wander to her ass.

"Joey Gracea," she turned back around with a book in her hand. "Is a famous author who used to be a therapist. He helped a sociopath who murder hundreds of women and men become a loyal citizen.

I mean, nevertheless he stayed in jail for the rest of his life. But Dr. Gracea, turned this mans life around, simply, by just talking to him," she sat back down. "And after hours of studying, analyzing, and talking to this man, Gracea found out, the reaosn why he was the way he was, was because his parents beat him," she handed me the book. "He wrote a book before he died, to future patients who might have a dirty family background." I took the book. "I would like for you to read it,"

I stared down a the thick book in my hands. I wanted to read it, and I knew I did. "I'll think about it," I looked up at her. "On one condition,"

"I'm not telling you my name," I chuckled.

"Whatever suits you. I like Vennessa anyways," she kept a nuteral face but I knew there were some thoughts swimming in that mind of hers. "Tell me what I said to you, that night I called," her eyes grew dark again as she bawled her hands into fist. She closed her eyes for a second and smiled.

"Something that helped me finish,"

Special

Dr. Morgan's POV

I groaned in satisfaction as I leaned my head back. My dopamine level is as high as when an addict smokes for the first time of the day. I turned off the recording and fixed my pants.

I grabbed a towel out of my drawer and cleaned up my mess. As I threw the towel in the basket that was in the corner of the room, my office door opened. I looked up to see Violet walking in with a smile. "If you needed help, I would have happily been at assist," she bit her bottom lip and I mentally rolled my eyes.

"I had enough help from Ms. Wilson's voice," I sat up straight and opened my computer. I could feel her eyes on me the entire time and I was tempted to yell at her but held back. The fact that I haven't fired her yet is surprising. Usually I only keep my receptionist until they get useless. Until their technique gets boring.

The only reason I'm keeping her for this long is because although I can't stand when she opens her mouth, it does wonders when it is open.

"Call Aaron and tell him I need those reports within the next five minutes," she didn't bother commenting on Ms. Wilson because she knew that she expendable. She silently nodded her head and left. I leaned forward on to my desk and sighed.

Vennessa.

I chuckled to myself as I recalled the name the innocent young'un called me. My name is something I keep sacred. Your name is how people refer to you, what they know about you, everything. Your name reveals more about you than you think. Something just as simple as your name is how people find out things about you that no one should know but you.

Even if I did tell someone my name, which I never will, they would have to be a hella of a person. The only people who know my name is my sister, unfortunately, and my parents. Only because they named me.

My door soon opened and quickly shut. I'd don't bother on looking up and just sighed. "What the hell did I tell you about coming into my office without asking?!" A file was slammed on my table and I looked up to seeAaron with a large grin.

"Read em and weep," I rolled my eyes and picked up the file. I looked through it to see pictures of the young girl with a redhead. They seemed close. A little too close.

I looked at the report to see the redhead was named Paige. 22, born in Kentucky, has a brother and mom who lives in England. Nothing seemed special about her.

Thoughts of what Olivia told me this afternoon hit me. "You're not special" I won't admit it and I never will but what she said hit something inside me. It was for a split second, to the point I didn't even know what it was at the moment.

"You don't ask for this kind of information about any of the other ones. What's so special about this girl?" I continued to look through the photos.

She was smiling in this one. Her teeth were perfectly straight and white. She appeared to look genuinely happy. I couldn't stop looking at her. She had brown eyes, which I never noticed, that just seemed to draw me in. She had a diamond pendant on her neck that had the letter A engraved. Her jawline was sharp, her body was curved in every right way, and her hair flowed flawlessly over her shoulders.

"Absolutely nothing,"

Not An Update

Should I add a little romance between Olivia and Mrs. Moore, or should I just keep it between Olivia and Dr. Morgan?

Angela and Venessa

I pulled up to the bar and got out of the cab. I need to really buy a car. But you know, broke college student. I'm surprised I'm not living on campus. And even if I couldn't afford my apartment I would just move in with Paige. Her family is like filthy rich apparently, which I just learned last month. And no doubt Paige would love to have a roommate.

I walked in and looked around to see not many people were here. But there was enough to make it seem crowded. I smiled as I saw Angela and walked over to her. "You wear that to a girl's night out," I whispered in her ear as I walked past. She looked up at me as I sat down and slightly smiled.

She waiter brought us four shots and two full glasses of something. I gave a confused smile as he handed me mine and walked away. I looked forward to see Angela grabbing a shot and downing it. "What the fuck-you're pregnant!" I yelled as I took the glass out of her hand. She laughed and shook her head.

"I might have lied about that. I just wanted to get you out here," I couldn't help but stare at her and roll my eyes. I could feel her eyes on me and in the back of my head I felt...that just maybe... never mind.

I nervously chuckled and scratched the side of my head, "well, ugh, is your husband actually out of town?" She downed another drink and I couldn't help but slightly lean forward again, the thought of her being pregnant still lingered in the back of my head, but I had to remember she wasn't.

She sighed as she put down the glass. "My husband and I are taking a break. Indefinitely," my face dropped a little as I slowly put my hand on hers.

"Angela, I am so sorry," she shook her head and I squeezed her hand. "I am more than happy to come out and spend time with you and make you feel better. You don't have to lie about it," she looked up at me and there was something in her eyes that looked familiar. It was the same look Dr. Morgan had in her eyes when I was in her office.

"Never thought I'd see you again," my heart started racing as I heard her voice from behind me. I turned my head to ironically see Dr. Morgan. But she wasn't talking to me. I looked forward to see Angela staring straight at her. I turned back around and Dr. Morgan's eyes were glued to Angela's face. The music was playing in the background making this situation even more...I don't even know the damn word for it.

Her hand was on the back of my chair and I could see her knuckles turning red. "HI, Venessa. Surprised to see you here," I said, trying to break the awkward silence. She slowly pulled her eyes away from Angela and looked at me. A smirk grew on her lips as she tilted her head.

"Venessa?" Angela said as she squinted her eyes in confusion.

"Seeing as she would not tell me her name, I thought it was only right to give her one," I said with a smile on my face. Angela slightly smiled back at me as if I was an innocent puppy. She looked back at Venessa and that smile turned into a snark.

"Is there a problem, Mrs. Moore? Or is it just Ms. now?" I could see how pissed Angela was getting by the twitch in her hand. Clearly, there is or was some type of history between them two, and although I'm a little interested in what that is, I would rather stay out of it.

"What, you've been keeping tabs on me? I thought you would be too occupied with your 'patients',?"

"Well, at least I'm not trying to screw someone younger than me because my crusty husband didn't want me anymore,"

"Yeah, you just like to screw younger women because you are a sadist who loves bending and manipulating young girls. And the only reason you do it is because deep down, you know, no one will ever love you," I watched as Venessa leaned forward onto the table and grinned.

"You did," Angela shifted in her seat and I could sense how much Venessa loved it. "You did love me, right?" She glared at her.

"Biggest mistake of my life," she gritted through her teeth. Venessa just chuckled and stood up. She put her hand on my shoulder

"Don't be naive Miss Wilson," she looked back at Angela. "She's just looking for someone to make her feel worthy," her eyes became dark. "It's pathetic," she let go of my shoulder and walked away. My eyes followed her all the way out the door. I turned back to the woman in front of me to see her messing with her hands.

"Are you-"

"I thought I told you to stay away from her!" I was taken aback by her tone but chose to ignore it seeing as this is clearly some type of crazy ex situation. Now, which one was the crazy one? I can probably guess who.

"Look I'm sorry. I just-"

"I'll see you tomorrow Olivia," she grabbed her purse and walked away. I groaned to myself. Not because I pissed her off but because I just wasted thirty bucks on a cab when I could have fucking been at home stuff my face with ice cream.

******

I feel like I'm moving a little too fast.

Eyes

Dr. Morgan POV

The sound of my pen continuously clicking was making my blood boil, even though I was the one clicking it. Maybe I should take a trip, go somewhere for a while. I scoffed to myself. I don't run away from things, nor people. They run from me. Seeing Angela brought up past memories. And those memories brought of past feelings. And those feelings brought up anger. I couldn't help but smile to myself as that woman actually believed I loved her.

I don't love anyone.

Even if I did feel more towards Angela than I did with anyone else, what I felt wasn't love. It was lust. Desire. The temptation never died. But she wasn't enough. What I had before her, what I did before I met her, it completed me. The power I hold over my patients. The way I can make them do anything I want, just by using words. It brings pleasure to my body. More than an orgasm ever has.

A knock on my door came and I looked up to see Violet. By the look in her eyes, I could tell why she's here. I have been avoiding her for the past few days and deep down I know why. But there was no way in hell I'm going to stop myself from getting a little pleasure because of some girl.

So I put on a smile and bit my bottom lip. This seemed to please her. "Good Morning. Your in early," it was six in the morning and she doesn't have to be here til eight. I only come in early because I basically live here. This place is my home away from home.

I have a back room in my office that is almost the size of my actual room at my house. I usually take people back there. My house is off limits. To me, my house is like my name. If you know it, then you know me. And no one knows me.

It's the mystery that makes things interesting.

"Just wanted to come see you, check up on ya," I grinned and leaned back in my chair. I put my fist under my chin and crossed my legs.

"Although, I know you lying," she looked down and blushed. "I can use a little cheering up," I motioned to her with my finger to come here and she happily obeyed.

I turned in my chair a little to the side as she bent down in front of me. I sat back and watched as she unzipped my pants. Her hand grabbed on to my cock with a strong grip. I could see the pleasure in her eyes as she started to stroke it. Her mouth opened, but before she could even do anything my office door opened.

"Gross," I clenched my hands into fist, tightly. Highly fucking annoyed. Violet let go, and I could see she was upset too.

"Aaron," I couldn't even muster up the words of what to say to him. I pushed back in my seat and turned around. Violet took the hint and stood up. She had her head down, feeling a little embarrassed causing me to roll my eyes. Women who have no grit in the themselves, no self respect repulse me.

She walked away and out the room without looking at Aaron. Aaron on the other hand didn't take her eyes off her until she closed the door behind her. "Why do you still have her?" He asked with disgust in is voice. Him and Violet actually used to date. I don't know what happened between them two, nor do I care. All I know is that she gives good head. Therefore, she stays.

I pushed back in my chair and gave a pissed off smile. "Would you like to do the honors instead?" He looked down then quickly looked away while groaning. I chuckled as I fixed my pants and buttoned them back up. "What do you want? And you got one more damn time to barge into my fucking office," he waved me off.

"Your threats don't work on me anymore you fucking whore," I rolled my eyes. Aaron is the closest thing I have to a friend. I don't consider him one. But again, close enough. "I just wanted to let you know your little...I don't even know what to call her. 'Next Target' doesn't seem fitting seeing as your making me stalk her,"

"I don't pay you to ask questions,"

"Well as much as I love getting paid, I do have a moral code. And hurting little innocent virgins is on my don't list," my eyes quickly met his.

"She's a virgin?" He squinted his eyes at me in confusion. He was trying to read me but failing. For some reason my mind blocked itself. My intentions with the girl faltered and I felt something. Something unusual. Something unwanted. I sat back in my chair and crossed my legs. Aaron titled his head a little when I did so. Crossing my legs is something that always throws him off.

Flexibility.

"Whoever said I wanted to hurt her?" He scoffed.

"The last time you sent me to do this much digging, that woman ended up face down in a ditch," I bit onto my bottom lip as images of my mother, if I can even call her that, came into my head. Aaron was still staring at me but I couldn't care less. I'm used to eyes always being on me. But what I don't like, is when those eyes aren't staring up at me.

"Well, I have no interest in hurting her. At least not in that way," I said. No doubt he could see the glint in my eyes. Aaron sighed and slightly nodded his head. "Now, leave. And please tell me receptionist to come back in here. She has unfinished business," there was something in his eyes as he looked at me. But it wasn't hatred.

I made sure before I hired Violet that she didn't have any sort of background that could affect me. It wasn't until after I hired her that I found out about them two. I was going to fire her but the bitterness he held in his eyes let me know that he was done with her. Plus her talents were good enough to make me forget about it.

Aaron left and Violet came back in. She shut the door behind her and quickly walked over to me. She had so much joy and lust in her eyes. And it wasn't until she knelt in front of me that it me.

She's not the one I want in front of me right now.

******

I'm sorry for these short ass chapters. My writers block is slowly deteriorating but it's still there.

Veronica

There was a time when life was pretty good. When I didn't have a care in the world. When I could go about my day and enjoy myself. And even if I had had a bad day, the next day, I forgot about it. Because back then, I was a dumb child who didn't have to worry about anything. I didn't know anything. I didn't know why my mother resented my father so much. I didn't know the way she looked at me wasn't with love or even pity. It was disgust.

I don't blame her though. I would say that I know what she's feeling or if I was put in her position, I would act the same way. But I wouldn't. Because if what happened to my mother happened to me and I got pregnant and I decided to keep the child, I would cherish it.

I would know that what happened to me wasn't their fault. I would look at them with love, I would protect them with life.

My mother did none of that. But my father did. Or at least he did in his own way.

Family is fucking confusing. And for that exact reason was why I left. I couldn't take the fighting or the yelling, or the way my head would spin every time I even thought about my childhood.

I sighed as I walked onto the porch and knocked on the door. I don't even know why I'm here. Her past is none of my business, but I'm fucking nosey so I had to.

The door opened and a depressed, tipsy, tired ass Angela opened the door. She was surprised to see me but didn't show it. I could smell the vodka from here and it stung my nose. "What are you doing here? More importantly, how do you know where I live?" I just shrugged my shoulders and she rolled her eyes.

"You weren't in class today. I was coming to check on you," I held up my arm. "And brought a peace offering," I held up a box of chocolate with a smile. She looked down at the box and considered it for a second. And for a moment there, I thought this would be the end of whatever problem she had with me. But by the look in her eyes, it was only the beginning.

"Why do you go to her?" I could see she was serious, but also in pain. I didn't have any words to say because I don't know why I still go to her. But I do. And there's no reasonable reason for it.

"I need a therapist. And she's a therapist. I'm sorry for whatever happened between you two but-"

"What happened between us!" She yelled. I slightly jumped back as she rubbed her head. "What she does, what she is," she covered her face with her hands and groaned. I wanted to reach out to her, she was in distress and I didn't know how to help. "Stay away from her,

Olivia. Please," I opened my mouth to say something but nothing came out.

She waved me off and stepped back. "Please," she shut the door and I crossed my arms. The signs are red. There's warning tape surrounding her. Every sign was pointed the other way. And yet, I keep going back.

I turned and walked away. Taxi's don't drive through here and a Cab would take too long. It was nearing 6 o'clock and the sun was slowly lowering. I decided to walk to my apartment to clear my head.

Our life is shaped by our mind, we become what we think. Joy follows a pure thought like a shadow that never leaves. Having a clear mind and a clear space allows you to think and act with purpose.

Life is too ironic to understand. It takes sadness to know what happiness is. Noise to appreciate silence, and absence to value presence. I live my life day by day, and I would like to keep it that way. Life is too precious to overthink everything.

I've been in my head for so long I didn't even know where I was walking. Have you ever been in that type of trance? When your writing, or walking, or even reading, and then you get in your head but you continue to do what you were doing just without knowing it? I didn't hit anyone or anything. I stopped at all the cross walking's, and yet, I don't even remember where I turned.

I sighed as I saw a coffee shop and went in. I don't even drink coffee.

The place was small and nice. Smelt good. I walked up to the counter and slightly smiled to myself as I saw they sell hot cocoa. I told the waiter and he nodded and went to go fix it.

What happened between Angela and Venessa that was so bad to the point it put Angela in distress like that just from seeing her? Venessa seems like an independent, strong, educated goddess- I mean woman. But I can't physically see her hurting someone.

But then again. I'm soft. I'm too precious. Too innocent. I've been told that my entire life. I'm a 21-year-old virgin for crying out loud. But being innocent and precious means being small. It means you are easily manipulated. And I hate that. I have been manipulated my entire childhood.

So you best believe I can see what Venessa is doing. And yet. I keep going back. I keep running into her hands. And if I think about it, it's because I see comfort in her. I see protection.

The waiter gave me my drink and I thanked him. I pulled out my wallet to pay but before I could, someone handed the man cash. "Allow me," I looked up and my eyes went big.

A woman with a bright smile and dark blonde hair, pouring over her shoulders, was smiling at me. The waiter took her money and I stepped back a little. "Thank you. You didn't have to do that," I said as I started to look down. I stopped myself from doing so though and cleared my throat. The woman continued to smile at me as if she knew what was going through my head.

"I wanted to," I chuckled a little as I looked around. Her eyes were still on me and I knew there was no chance of me just leaving.

"Ugh, how can I repay you? I could buy you something," I said gesturing towards the menu.

"Well, that would just defeat the purpose of me paying for you now wouldn't it?" Her voice was so fucking soothing. It wasn't rough but it wasn't soft either. It's like the words just perfectly flowed off her tongue. "A walk would suffice if you would like," she tilted her head forward a bit and I nodded. Her smile soon came back as we walked outside. She opened the door for me and I walked past her.

We started down the street, that now that I think about it, have never been on. "So, I feel like we should start off with something simple. What's your name?" She asked.

"Olivia,"

"Pretty name for a pretty girl," I couldn't stop the smile from creeping onto my lips so I drank my cocoa to hide it. But that couldn't stop my blush from appearing.

"You?"

"Veronica," I nodded my head. That was a pretty name but I didn't want to say back what she said to me. That's fucking weird. And beyond stupid.

"So Veronica," she slightly laughed. "You live around here?" She sighed as she put her hands into her pockets.

"No. I live in France. I'm just visiting some family," I nodded again.

"France. Long way from home," she shook her head.

"I'm actually from the U.S. I just left because, of well, the same reason why I'm visiting," I chuckled.

"Family is hard. I understand stand that more than anyone," I could see her side-eye me. Most people do. But the way she did it was different. As if she had all the answers to my problem.

"Family is an interesting and hard concept. We were taught as children that family is blood and deep bonds we make with people. And that those bonds and that blood are supposed to hold together no matter what. That parents are supposed to be the bigger person in an argument and take fault, admit they're wrong even if they're not. That you have to stick up for the people you share blood with. That even if they do something to you that hurts you physically and/or mentally we're supposed to stay together. Fight then forgive. But the fact of the matter is. That's not true. Just because you share DNA with someone, doesn't give them the right to anything. Just because your parents made you, doesn't give them the right to hurt you. Sometimes family is the cruelest form of love there is, for no one can hurt you more than the people who created you. Sometimes blood is as thick as water," her words went into my head and stayed there.

I have known this woman for less than ten minutes and I already feel a deeper connection with her than I have with anyone. She soon came to a stop and so did i.

As I looked at her something happened. Something intimate. But it wasn't that. It was the fact that those eyes seemed too familiar. I must have been staring too long and too intensively because she started smiling. "I have to go catch up with that family visit now. But I do hope to see you again Olivia," I started blushing as I looked down at the cup in my hand. "I am a little old fashion, so I do believe it's a little too early to ask for your number. So instead, I will tell you that tomorrow, at this exact time, I will be in that coffee shop. And if I just so happened to run into you, my day would be ten times better," I looked back up at her and nodded my head while trying to hide my smile. "Until then," she pretended to tilt a hat, making me laugh.

Both of us turned and walked away. Of course, I had to turn around to see where she was going, and when I did, I caught her watching me too. But she didn't look away. Instead, she winked at me. I turned back around and continued to walk, my face bright red.

Third-person POV

Veronica was slightly smiling to herself as she watched the girl walk away. She was so small and fragile. She wanted her.

She sighed though as she walked into the building. She hates this place more than anything. She doesn't even know why she's here. She has made a life for herself in France. Although the young girl did make her trip worthwhile, she would rather be back across the country. She rode up the elevator, annoyed before she even sees anyone.

She hated her parents and didn't want to be like either of them. But small patience and a bad temper are something she inherited, just runs through the family. She stepped out of the elevator and rolled her eyes. "So dramatic" she thought.

She walked towards the doors and opened them. She saw the other woman coming out of the backroom and knew exactly what was either happening or about to happen.

The other woman looked up, sensing another presence. Multiple emotions crossed her face but only one seemed to stick. Anger. Annoyance. "And to what do I owe this pleasure?" The other woman asked. Veronica chuckled as she shook her head.

"Just thought I'd drop by. Especially after hearing all the great things about Dr. Morgan, and how her words and methods are so efficient and memorizing," the other woman chuckled mockingly as she went to go sit down at her desk. She leaned back and grinned.

"Nice to know I'm known, even across the globe," Veronica crossed her arms. "So again I ask," the other woman leaned forwards. "To what do I owe the pleasure," Veronica walked towards the woman and sat down in one of the other chairs in front of her desk.

"What? I can't come say hi to my big sister?"

*****

My glorious writing is back bitch!!!

Sisters

I am on a fucking role today. I just wrote all this in ten minutes

******

Dr. Morgan's POV

I got everything ready in the backroom of my office and looked around to make sure everything was set. I started to scratch my arm as my nerves started to get to me. There is a side of me that rarely comes out, and for some reason, it's out now.

I couldn't stop scratching my arm and it got to the point I didn't even know I was doing it. I started hyperventilating a little, and it wasn't until I started feeling pain in the area I was scratching, that I took back control of my body and focused on my breathing.

My doctor tells me that I have anxiety attacks and that I need to start taking medicine for it. I would rather be buried alive six feet underground in Antarctica than to be on medication.

I closed my eyes and straightened myself. I cleared my throat along with my head and moved back into my office. I closed the door behind me, and made sure I didn't lock it.

I lifted my head when I sensed a presence. I turned around with a smile, expecting my patient, but instead, I can face to face with one of the two last people on this earth I didn't want to see.

Not going to lie, for a moment there I was almost happy to see her. Then I was confused. But in the end, I pissed. She has no right to be here. We all went our separate ways the day we were legally allowed to drive. Smiled as she crossed her arms. "And to what do I owe this pleasure?" I asked. She shrugged her shoulders.

"Just thought I'd drop by. Especially after hearing all the great things about Dr. Morgan, and how her words and methods are so efficient and memorizing," I went to go sit down at my desk and leaned back with a giant grin.

"Nice to know I'm known, even across the globe," I leaned forward onto my desk. "Now again I ask, to what do I owe the pleasure?" Veronica walked towards me and say down in the chair in front of me. She crossed her legs and smiled.

"What? I can't come say hi to my big sister?" She knew calling me her sister would upset me. I like to believe I have no family. That I started my line and I will end it with me. That's how I've always been even as kids. At some point though, I did try to be her big sister, but I couldn't. Our parents favored her over me so damn much. And yet, she complained that she hated them. I grew up despising her, resenting her. She had everything and acted as if she had nothing.

I learned very quickly at a young age that I am all that matters. No one will look after me like I will. No one would care for me as I do. So I stopped caring about people. I didn't dare go out and look for relationships. I stayed to myself. I got to know myself. And once I figured all that out, I was unstoppable.

At that point in time, I had respect from everyone. They either feared me or wanted to do everything I told them to do. I had the looks, I had the charm, I had the dominance.

And so did Veronica.

But one thing that set me up above her, that put me on higher grounds, was what was between my legs. And although that ruined the relationship I had with my parents, it made every woman I've ever met begging at my feet.

And I would take this life over anything Veronica has any day.

"How's France?" I asked. She snorted.

"Do you care?"

"No," she rolled her eyes. We share very similar features. But in reality, we look nothing alike. We have the same nose, the same ears, the eyes. But we have two different personalities.

In high school, she had all the friends, all the fame, all the love. But she didn't care about that. She only cared about her girlfriends. And she had multiple. But she wasn't a player. She just loved too easily. She would get with a girl, they would go on dates, post idiotic couple pictures, send one another valentine gifs. But at the end of the day she left all of them. You would think by the way she treated every single one of them she was truly in love. But nope.

She would love and cherish one girl for two months, then all of a sudden dump her, and act as if she never existed.

Me on the other hand, I made each and every single one of them remembered me. I always had them doing things for me. My homework, carrying my bag, other things. I had each and every single one eating out the palm of my hand. I would give special attention to one at a time, then once I grew tired with them I moved on to the next.

I never cared for any of them. Half of em had boyfriends. But none of them could please them the way I could.

Veronica and I were known as the ordeñadoras mami sisters. I think during that time in our lives, we were so consumed in our own world that we didn't pay attention to anyone or anything else. We buried ourselves in those girls to escape what was happening at home.

And once we graduated, Veronica moved to France to start a new life, and I moved to Virgina. Honestly, the main reason why I picked Virgina was because it looked like Vagina.

"Dad called. Said he wanted us all together," I scoffed and slightly threw my head back.

"You came all the way down here, just to tell me that. Knowing damn well I'ma not going. You and your entire family can kiss my ass," I stood up and walked over to my bookshelf.

"He's burring mom next week and asked us to be there," I didn't respond and started looking through the shelf. "He called my office 172 times V. He's desperate,"

"He can die along mom for all I care," I picked up the book I was looking for and walked back to my desk.

"You are the reason mom died!" I stopped walking and turned to face her. I slammed the book against the desk and slowly walked towards her.

"You think, after damn near 20 years, you can show up at my doorstep and make demands?" I asked quietly, but she could hear the anger in my voice. Veronica has nothing on me when it comes to who's boss. And she knows that. She held her head high up though. No doubt, she's used to being the one giving orders. "Your in my domain now. You don't tell me what to do. And mom died because and incompetent woman incapable of loving anyone but herself,"

Veronica shook her head while never breaking eye contact. "And who does that remind you of?" We stared at one another for quite some time. In the end, I remembered the day I had ahead of me and walked away. "Well at least my trip wasn't a complete lost,"

I sat down at my desk and looked at her. "I have a date tomorrow," I snorted and rolled my eyes.

"Of course you do. Am I to expect to see her at the funeral?" She shrugged her shoulders.

"Maybe, we'll see," I shook my head at her. Imbecile. Love fades. And it dies. I don't know how long it's going to take her to see that.

Date

After you read the last sent, come back up and play this song

******

I don't know whether I was hyped up or ready to fucking die. I was so ready to leave but also wished time would slow down. I was excited, no doubt in that, but I was also nervous. I haven't been on a date since 10th grade. I don't even know if I can call this a date. I mean, Veronica seemed interested in me. She's a very beautiful woman, and I'm surprised she even gave me a second glance. And by that I mean she seems to be the person to date someone mature, someone who's already started their life. Maybe she doesn't know how old I am. I tend to look older. But then again, when she saw me, I looked bat shit stupid.

My hair wasn't done. I wasn't wearing any make-up. I'm pretty sure I was sweaty. Like, why the fuck would she pay for me?!

All these thoughts and doubts kept swarming in my head to the point I didn't even hear the bell ring. I sighed as I got up from my chair and grabbed my bag. "You weren't paying attention the entire time," I looked up to see Mrs, well I guess Ms, now, Moore looking at me.

I slightly chuckled and held onto my bag. "Deep in thought. You know me," she nodded her head a little and I slowly approached her. "I heard what you said yesterday," she looked up at me. "If you really think I shouldn't go see her anymore, I'll find someone else," she looked down at her feet.

"I'm sorry about yesterday. I was too wrapped up in my own emotions and took them out on you. I apologize," I smiled and nodded my head. "I don't have any meetings today. If you want, I can make it up to you, buy you a drink or something," I held up my hand and shook my head.

"No need. I actually have a somewhat date today anyways," I watched as she smirked and moved to the front of her desk and sat down on it.

"Interesting. Does she go here?" I shook my head no.

"I hope not. But you know, the world is small. Next thing you know we go out and the next day I find out she's my new history teacher," we both laughed.

"Well text me how it goes," I nodded my head and started to walk away. "And tell Paige she needs to fucking turn in her essay. It was due two weeks ago," I snorted.

"I've never even seen that girl write her own name,"

****

I went through my closet hundreds of times trying to find the right outfit. Is this a dress up type thing? Where we meet up at the coffee shop and then go somewhere fancy? Or is this a look cute but comfortable type thing? I hated myself seeing as I'm overthinking my clothes.

I scratched my head and looked over my closet. After twenty minutes of sitting there looking stupid, I decided on some blue jeans and a cut out ruched t-shirt. This is my favorite shirt because it my makes my boobs look bigger.

I rarely wear it because it does shape me a lot but it's not really my thing. I kept rethinking it because Veronica might think I'm trying too hard. I hurried up and grabbed my keys and purse before I could start to hate it.

I locked my door and made my way outside.

After Veronica had left, I walked back up the street and found out what the coffee shop was called. I looked on my Google maps and decided just to walk, seeing it was five minutes away.

What my dumbass didn't realize was that that five minutes was by car. By foot, is 10-15 minutes.

I don't know why the fuck I didn't call a cab once I realized that. I kept telling myself that I already started, might as well finish it. The coffee shop came into view and I weakly smiled. I really need to get back in the gym. I look good but I can't run for more than a minute and a half straight.

I opened the door and went in. I looked around the place and didn't see her. Immediately my mind started playing tricks on me but I blocked it out. I walked over to one of the booths and sat down. I would order a cup of tea to pass the time but I didn't want to spend my money if I wasn't staying. "You look beautiful," I slightly jumped as I looked up to see those green eyes that remind me of something. Or someone. I just can't seem to put my finger on it.

Veronica was smiling at me while slightly looking me over. She tired to hide what she was doing by looking over my shoulder but it didn't work. She was wearing something casual so my nerves slightly went away. "Thank you. You don't look to bad yourself," she chuckled and sat down across from me.

"It's been a while since I've been able to wear something so unpretentious. In my line of work I have to wear clothes that show power. And then have to do fundraisers to then I have to wear something elegant. And when I'm not working I still have to show that power because I always have eyes on me," I nodded as I leaned back.

"And that brings me to the question, what is it that you do?"

"Neuro Surgeon," I stared at her in awe and mentally started punching myself. A fucking Neuro Surgeon. Who lives in England. And constantly has eyes on her. The amount of stupidity I feel right now just talking to her.

"Is that why you knew so much about family issues yesterday?" She crossed her arms and leaned forward onto the table.

"A little. But that was more of experience than knowledge. Family issues is more of my sister's area of expertise," I hummed in response. "When I first started I wanted to work in general surgery. But as time went by and I started to learn more, the human brain just fascinated me more and more everyday," I slightly grinned.

"So you know some things about the human body?"

"I know a lot of things about the human body," I watched as she bit her bottom lip and I couldn't help but look down and blush. "You are so cute," I started regretting not buying a drink cause I can't hide behind it.

I cleared my throat and looked back up at her. The glint in her eyes wasn't just lust. It was pure enlightenment. I've never had someone look at me like that. And for that exact reason was why I realized who she reminded me of. "Your sister, the one who specializes in family issues," I watched as the look in her eyes slightly went away. "What's her name?"

Before she could say anything her phone started to ring. She looked at me apologeticly and I waved her off. I opened my phone to make it seem like I wasn't listening to her conversation. "Yes I'm still here. Why? Because dad asked so. V, I don't want to go either but at least-. You know what, don't go or do, I seriously couldn't careless at this point," she started rubbing her forehead with her other hand as if she had a headache. "I would come over but it's not like I know where you fucking live," I couldn't help but stiff a laugh and that made her look over at me. She started smiling and shook her head. "Yes I am on my date right now," I couldn't help but smile to myself. "So if I bring her you'll go?"

Veronica's POV

"So if I bring her you'll go?" I asked.

"Yes, I want to see who your next victim is. She must be something if you didn't fuck her the moment you saw her," I rolled my eyes.

"That's your think, not mine," she started to laugh her annoying as laugh that would scare people back in high school.

"Uh yes, I forgot. Fucking and ditching is my thing. You talk and talk and play the nice guy. Then you fuck and go on dates and fuck again. And then you leave. As much as you hate to admit it Veronica, we do the exact same thing. My way is just quicker and more pleasant," I wanted to reach into this phone and strangle the shit out of her.

But whenever I looked over, I saw Olivia scrolling through her phone, trying to act as if she wasn't listening. Something about her just seems so intriguing. "I'll call you later V. Or not. Hearing your voice makes me want to cut out my brain,"

"Whatever," she hung up the phone. Always so damn dramatic. I sighed as I put my phone down on the counter.

"You okay?" I nodded my head and looked down at the girl. She is so petite it almost makes me afraid to touch her. Almost.

"Perfectly fine, but unfortunately, I do have to cut our time short," she nodded and looked away. I could see the disappointment in her eyes. I stood up and she followed. As she leaned to grab her purse, I couldn't control myself as I slithered my arm around her waist and kissed her.

I could feel her tense up but after a few seconds she slowly relaxed. By the amount of time she took to relax gave me the conclusion that she hasn't kissed anyone in a while. Or maybe, this might be her first kiss. Which that couldn't be. She's way to damn pretty to not have kissed someone.

I slowly pulled back, taking her bottom lip with me. I could feel her shaking and that made me smile. "That wasn't very old fashion of you," she whispered. I somewhat laughed and my grip around her waist tightened. With my other hand, I ran my fingers through her hair.

"Couldn't help myself I guess," she started blushing which is something she tends to do very often. "I'll see you around, love," I removed my arm from around her waist. I pulled a pen out my back pocket and wrote down my number. I gave it to her and winked as I slowly turned around and walked away.

I started laughing to myself. I wonder how my sister would feel about me taking one of her patients off her hands.

Patient, Patience

"Taking care of yourself is not selfish or egocentric but essential to finding your own success. Finding balance begins with allowing yourself the opportunity to build a foundation of how you want others to see you. Feeling compassion for ourselves in no way releases from responsibility for our actions. Rather it releases us from the self hatred the prevents us from responding you our life with clarity and balance. Each of us secretly and desperately yearns to be recognized for our own uniquenesses, our fullness, and our vulnerability. We yearn to be genuinely valued by others for who we are.

Instead of adding to your anxiety by being mean to yourself abate to it by giving yourself the same kind words you give to others."

I closed the book as the chapter ended. It is a good book, and somewhat inspiring. But I don't see this author changing a murderous homicidal man into a good citizen.

I had decided to give Venessa's therapy book a hand. Although I will nerve admit it to her, it wasn't that bad. After every chapter I had sat there and thought about what it was saying, and put those words into my past.

Also, it took my mind off of Veronica. When she kissed me yesterday I froze. It wasn't my first kiss but it felt like it. The fire I felt inside of me, the yearning I had for more when she pulled away. Everything just seemed so different, but yet. There was something off.

I don't know what it was, or if it was just my mind playing tricks with me. I wanted her. Like, badly. But there was something pulling me in another direction. A complete different one.

I knew what it was. But I didn't like it. Nor did I understand it. Why would someone who is not doubt playing with me, stopping me from pushing forward with what's right in front of me? I don't even know the woman's name, and yet the thought of her lives in the back of my mind.

She's very secretive, mysterious. And maybe it's that. Maybe I see a mystery I want to solve. Maybe if I solve it, I won't think of her that much. Hopefully none at all. But solving a mystery that no one seems to have solved before is a terrible place to start.

Well. Maybe someone has.

Angela and Venessa dated. And from the looks of it, Angela was in love with her. Maybe in the time frame of them "together", she learned her name. I sat there while biting my lip, deep in thought. I don't want to upset Angela though by asking about Venessa.

I looked at the clock by bed and saw that my first class was in about an hour.

I decided to head in early to see if I can catch Angela before school starts. Waking up at 9 in the morning should be an easy thing to do. Which it is. But getting out of bed is different criteria.

My adrenaline to find out these things were the only thing that got me up. I did all my bathroom routines. No need to go into detail about that. I grabbed my stuff and left.

When I got to school the place was empty. Only a few professors roamed the halls. All of them looked like they were, happy. Like that actually enjoyed their life's. I guess the peace and and quiet made them sane. They are usually yelling at us up and down. I don't blame them though, half the people here are annoying as hell. I don't even know why they come.

I went to Angela's class and quietly knocked. I poked my head in to see her at her desk. She looked up and smiled. "Hey, your early," I closed the door behind me and sat my bag on one of the desk.

"Just wanted to come and hang out...and other things," she leaned back in her chair and crossed her arms. She squinted her eyes at me as if she didn't believe. I don't blame her for it.

I started messing with my hands as I walked towards her. I don't know how to start because I don't want to just straight up ask her. I started debating with myself if I should even ask her. It's a sensitive topic that she no doubt wants to talk about.

But the way that this woman kept my mind occupied haunted me. "Olivia. You okay?" I cleared my throat and looked around the classroom.

"Uh, yeah. I'm just," once I turned to look at her my words spilled out my mouth before I could even process it. "What's Dr. Morgan's first name?" I immediately regretted asking it as I watched her smile disappear faster than it came.

I started scratching the back of my hand as I could feel her eyes on me. "Why do you care. So much. About her?" There was a sense of pain and anger mixed in her voice. I stuttered upon my words as I wrapped my arms around myself. The way her eyes pierced through mine. The hate that visibly showed, pained me. But before I could even apologize the door opened. And when I freaking tell. Worst. Timing. Ever!

My breath got caught in my throat as she stared at me. "What are you doing here?" I managed to say. The only reason I was so caught up in my words was because of Angela. I just brought of memories for her and then next thing you know, the cause of this memories appears.

"Heard my name. Thought I pop in," she turned her head to look at Angela. "Hi beautiful," she winked at her and Angela took a sharp breath in. I cleared my throat and grabbed my bag. I feel obligated to stay but I don't want to. "Matter of fact, I actually came by to talk to you,"

Angela's eyes snapped towards me. I squinted in confusion. "Olivia's busy. Leave or-"

"Or what?" Venessa snapped. I couldn't help but slightly jump back, but Angela didn't move an inch. They stared one another down. It was quiet for a while and I couldn't stand it. So I just walked out the door.

People have problems. People have a past. Hell, I have a past. And I know I keep saying this, that I shouldn't barge into their lives, but I did. And I know I shouldn't have. But my curiosity took over me. My selfishness took over me.

I walked into the bathroom and threw my bag on the floor. It was still too early for anyone to be here. I groaned and covered my face with my hands. I turned on the water and splashed my face.

I heard the door open and close. And then I heard it lock.

I wiped my face of the water and reached for a paper towel. Once I dried my face I opened my eyes and screamed. Venessa was standing behind me with her arms cross. Staring.

I looked at her through the mirror. I didn't want to turn around. I don't know what was running through me. It wasn't fear. But I was afraid.

That makes no sense.

"I like to take my time with my patients," she was staring straight at me now through the mirror. "When I first became a therapist, I was straight forward. I didn't really care about any of them. I just wanted pleasure. I wanted power," she moved off the wall. "But as time went by, my knowledge grew. My hunger, for dominance grew. Now, I have patience. I get to know my patients. I get to know what makes them weak. What brings them to their knees," she walked towards me. "I. Am patient," I stiffened as her front came in contact with my back. She leaned down to where her mouth was right next to my ear. "But I don't want to be patient with you," before I could even comprehend what was happening, she turned me around and kissed me.

Hard.

Her hands were gripping my waist tightly and her lips were pressed against mines. My mind was swarming with thoughts, but I couldn't focus. Cause I didn't want to.

Cause I felt content.

I felt as if something that has been weighing me down for so long, was lifted up.

I felt as if a weight was lifted off my shoulders.

She slowly pulled away, bringing my bottom lip with her. Her hands traveled up my body as she kissed me again. I felt her tongue run against my bottom lip but she didn't give me a chance to accept it.

Her mouth moved to my neck. I opened my mouth to moan but instead, a squeal came out as she bit down. "I know you're seeing someone," she moved her knee in between my legs. I held myself up against the counter sink. "I don't know who, nor for I care," her voice got more aggressive with each passing word. "All I know, is that they better not touch you,"

I was so seduced by her words I didn't even feel her hand move into pants.

I jerked back as I felt an unfamiliar feeling flow through my body. "A flower isn't meant to be ruined. It should be treasured, kept safe, protected," her finger started making circular figures and my mouth gaped opened. She took my lip in hers and bit down hard.

I felt the blood run down my throat. "I can pleasure you in more ways than you can imagine," I yelled as I felt her finger enter inside me. "So tight. So pure," she whispered.

She took her finger out of me and out my pants. I fell down to my knees and put my hand in between my legs, feeling my wetness sink through my pants. She bent down in front of me and grabbed my chin with her hand and made me look at her. "No one touches you. Am I clear, Olivia?" I was too stunned to say anything. She stood up and my eyes dropped.

She looked at where my gaze was and smiled. "Like I said. I can please you in more ways than you can imagine," the look that crossed her face of me on my knees in front of her made her smile. "And clearly, looking at you so sexually frustrated, and helpless, pleases me," my breathing was heavy as I looked up at her. She winked at me and walked away.

I heard the door unlock and open then close. I leaned back against the wall and closed my eyes.

"Fuck,"

Lots of Firsts

Penis, penis, penis. Penis.

That's literally all I could think about. And I'm gay! I couldn't focus on her hands, or how they held onto my hips, or how her eyes held so much freaking dominance and lust, or how my lip is bruised, I can't even focus on the damn kiss. The only thing that occupied my mind was the word penis.

"Like I said. I can please you in more ways than you can imagine, and clearly, looking at you so sexually frustrated, and helpless, pleases me"

Ok, other than the fact this woman clearly has a degrading kink, what does she mean by that? I mean, I know what she meant. Deep down, I know what she meant. But it was like there was something blocking me from even finishing that thought.

I can't come to a conclusion about something unless I have all the facts. And at the moment, I have a few facts. But I don't have enough evidence. I mentally scoffed. What? You want her to pull down her pants and show you?

Everything about this woman is so frustrating! Her actions and her emotions, if I can even call them that. No. It's not even her emotions, it's mines. I can't control them. I can't stop them. I can't see that this woman in clearly just using just like she apparently does to other people. I'm just a means to an end to her.

"Are you okay, love?" I snapped out of thought as I looked up to see a smiling Veronica looking concerned. I cleared my throat and nodded my head. She continued to stare at me, not doubt, knowing I'm lying. But instead of pushing on it she grabbed my hand. I looked down and a small blush couldn't help but pop up.

I heard Veronica giggle. "I like when you do that," I nervously pulled away my hand and looked back at the water fountain.

We were at the park and after a few minutes of walking around aimlessly she got a call. So I went to go sit down at this bench that was in front of a fountain. I always loved fountains. Especially around Christmas time. When people would decorate it, and the color of water would change, and people would come together take pictures around it.

But at the moment, it was just a plain water fountain, but it still put a smile to my face. "What was the call about? If you don't mind me asking," she leaned back and crossed her arms and legs. She had on sunglasses and was staring around at the people walking around.

"My sister," she sighed after she said it. Making the conclusion that her and her sister don't get along too well. "My mother's burial is coming up soon, and my father wanted both of his daughters there," I nodded my head.

"Does she not want to go?" I asked. I know my mother and I have a past, but like, if she died, I would go to her funeral.

"Our family doesn't get along too well. Especially my sister. She's independent. Has been for as long as I can remember," I could hence the sadness in her voice. But there was also anger in it. "All I wanted growing up was a sister. And I had one. But to her, I wasn't her sister. I was just a random person living down the hall from her. And I'll be honest, it hurt," I reluctantly put my hand on her lap, not knowing what to say. She looked down at my hand and grinned. "But as we got older, I learned a lesson. Family isn't everything," she turned to look at me. "Sometimes blood is as thick as water,"

My face dropped a little as I remember hearing that from somewhere. Or someone, but I can't remember where. "Can I confess something to you?" I nodded my head and watched as she started smiling. "I can't stop thinking about the kiss we had," I started nervously chuckling and smiled brightly.

"I haven't been able stop replying it in my head," as she started laughing, it occurred to me. It wasn't her kiss that's been on my mind all day. Once I realized that, I knew I had to go. "Um, this has been really great, but I have a test that I need to study for tomorrow," she didn't say anything for a hot second, and because of her sunglasses, I couldn't tell how she was reacting. Before I could say anything else she smiled and stood up.

She held out her hand and I took it. I thought she was just helping me stand up, but when I did stand up she pulled me into her and grabbed my face and kissed me. As last time, I was taken off guard.

Her lips were so damn soft, and I could feel that she wanted more but controlled herself. My lips found her pace and I flowed with it. She slowly slipped her tongue into my mouth and that's when I started to panic. I didn't know what I was doing and we're in the middle of a freaking park. The kiss lasted for a heated minute and when she pulled back I could feel the heat on my cheeks. "Sorry," she whispered while slightly panting. "Just had to make sure I wasn't losing you," she moved my hair out my face with a slightly grin on her lips.

"No, no it's not that. I-its just that I-I never-"

"Was that your first kiss?" She asked with a sense of curiosity and humor. I started backing up a little and put my hands behind back. I guess my silence gave her her answer. When I looked up at her, it's like confirmation formed in her head and a smile started to slowly form. "You are so damn precious," she whispered to herself.

The word triggered me a little and I cleared my throat. "Uh, I'll text you later," I started to back away and it's like something just took over her. She never moved but I could see the way her eyes changed. They went from that sweet beautiful green, to eyes full of lust and hunger. And there was not one ounce of doubt of where I've seen those eyes.

I turned away from her and walked back to where we came from. I was too pissed off to even realize how fast I was going. And next thing you know, I'm in the elevator.

My nerves were up so high, all the investigation I had planned went out the window. I wanted answers and I wanted them now. Once the elevator doors opened I went straight to her office, ignoring the whorish receptionist telling me to stop. I forcibly open her doors, only to see her in her chair, staring straight at me, as if she knew I was coming.

"Good afternoon Miss Wilson. We really should get you on a scheduled time," I could feel the receptionist presence behind me so I shut the door in her face. I watched as she closed her eyes and chuckled to herself.

"Is this some type of game to you? Am I some type of game to you?!" My voice started rising with each passing word. I watched as she just sat there and stared.

"Can you be a little more specific?" She asked in a calm voice. I put my hand to my forehead and took a few breaths before I started yelling and end up just looking like a child.

"I hate myself. I hate myself for how easily manipulated I can be. People take the innocence I have and play with it. They use it for their own amusement, as if what they do doesn't take an effect on me and I fell for it again twice in the last week!" Her facial expression didn't change. But her eyes did.

"So, you read the book," I wanted to bang my head against a wall.

"Why did you show up at my school? Why did you corner me in the bathroom? Why did you kiss me? What did you mean you can pleasure me in more ways than one?" So many questions were running through my head and not having answers was driving me out my mind.

"I can't answer any of those questions-"

"Why the hell not?!" My hands were bawled into fist as she looked down at her own hands, as if contemplating what she should do.

"Are you here as my patient, or as a personal matter?" She asked as she got out of her chair. I watched as she walked towards me. Today she was in a suit. A very alluring, seductive suit that seemed to make my mouth water. "Please answer Miss Wilson before I become irritated," I cleared my throat.

"Personal," she nodded her head and walked up to me. With each step she took forwards I wanted to take five backwards.

"I showed up to your school because I couldn't stop thinking about you. I cornered you in the bathroom because I wanted to see how you would react to have someone stand over you, and watch you squirm until you fell to your knees," she was standing directly in front of me now. "I kissed you because I had been wanting to do that since the moment I laid eyes on you. I wanted to know how your lips would quiver under mine. How they would part as I stuck my hands in between your legs and circled your clit. And as for the last thing," she ran her hand through my hair and pulled my head back. Her lips went to my ear, "you knew exactly what I meant," a whimper left my mouth as she started nibbling on my ear.

"I'm going to fuck you now Miss Wilson," I felt my inside starting to burn as she ran her tongue down my neck. She started sucking on my collarbone making my knees go weak. "And if I'm being honest," she moved back up to my neck and once her tongue touched that spot a moan slipped out mouth. This seemed to arouse her as her grip on my hair tightened. "I haven't felt this excited to fuck someone in a while,"

******Not me literally listening to Chase Atlantic right now and not adding a s*x scene.

Not Like This

Just started watching Euphoria.

I have no words

****

Her lips were on my neck. There was a tingling feeling running through my body. Every bone, muscle, and all my sense were on alert.

When certain parts of our bodies are touched, certain enzymes and chemicals that trigger sexual desire are released into our systems. The more our bodies simulated, the more chemicals are released and the greater our sexual desire grows until it becomes virtually unstoppable flood.

Her hands roamed up and down my body. She would squeeze my skin every once in a while as if making sure I was real.

She pushed me up against her desk and leaned her body on to mine. I wrapped my leg around her waist and she grabbed it. A small squeal left my mouth once she started biting down my neck again. Her breathing started to get heavy but her actions were slowing down.

I thought she was going to kiss me again, but instead, her mouth just hovered on mine. She pressed her center against mine, confirming my suspicion. A quiet moan left my mouth and to that, her grip tightened against my leg.

She wanted to do more. I wanted to do more, and she knew that. But she didn't do anything. She leaned her head against mine with her eyes close. "It shouldn't be like this," she whispered. I was confused and frustrated because I wanted to be touched. I wanted everything.

She hesitantly let go of my leg while shaking her head. When she opened her eyes we were both staring at one another. She looked me up and down and I could see within her eyes that she wanted me. The lust that was in them clearly stated it.

But once she looked back up at me, I watched as that lust slowly turned into fear. I squinted my eyes trying to figure out what was wrong but she quickly looked away.

I got off the desk as she walked to a door that was across from her couch. And now that I think about it, I've never noticed it.

She put her hand on the doorknob but didn't open it. She was looking at the ground then she looked over at me. "What?" I asked quietly. She opened her mouth to say something but nothing came out. I soon recognized the look in her eyes.

Pity.

I bit my bottom lip and looked at my feet with my arms behind my back. "Sorry to waste your time," I said and walked away.

"Olivia," I stopped as my name left her mouth. She rarely calls me by my first name. I turned back to look at her but she continued to stay silent.

"Is it me? Or, do you just not want to anymore? Was the game to mess with me and get me turned on, then at the last second throw me away?! Because you and your sister-"

"I don't have a sister," she said. I threw my hands up.

"What do you mean? I know-"

"I do not have any family, Olivia. Whoever this person your referring to is, is not related to me," I started rubbing my forehead getting the biggest headache. At some point I had had enough and opened the door. "Your first time shouldn't be on some desk by a woman who doesn't care about you, Olivia," I had paused as her words hit me.

At least she confirmed it. She doesn't care about me. I mentally slapped myself because I already knew that.

I closed the door behind me and left. Maybe I should just sell my virginity online. At least then I'll get paid for it.

Dr. Morgan's POV

I sat there staring at the door. Why didn't I take her? Why did I stop? Why the fuck did I say that?! I should be her first. She would never forget me if I did. I would stay on her mind forever. Every time she thought about her first time she would think about me.

I would be that special someone to her.

But the feeling that ran through my body when I thought about that stopped me from doing it. When she moaned in my ear I could sense how vulnerable she was. She wanted someone to please her. She wanted someone to treat her body the way she needed it. The way she craved it.

Every night for the past week in a half I have dreamed about fucking her. I wanted her so damn bad. I wanted to know how her pussy would squeeze around cock, how her lips would feel against my skin, I wanted to know every inch of her skin.

I moved my hips in a circle as I felt my dick starting to throb. My phone ding on the table and I grabbed it.

VeronicaI'll be there at 10 a.m. You better be packed and fucking ready. I'm not joking.

I scoffed and rolled my eyes. I don't want to go to this fucking burial. None of my family ever liked me nor do I like them. My aunt's my uncle's my cousins, all of them hated me growing up. Now, did I give one shit?

No.

But, one thing I can always count of Veronica to do is bug the hell out of me until I go. Honestly, that's the only decent thing I like about her. She's persistent. Dedicated. I'll give her that.

I got out of my chair and grabbed my keys. In all honesty. I just want to see who her new play to is.

Asking

I don't want to prof read. You know what the fuck I meant.

*****"

About time school was out I was totally drained and exhausted. I had took four test today and Ms. Moore had us write, type, and edit a five page paper all in one class period. I could sense she was upset. It wasn't the fact that she made us do all this stuff. I mean, she's a college professor, she's supposed to give us this type of work. But it was her tone and her attitude that made me get the impression she wasn't having it today

I haven't talked to her since that day Venessa kissed me. Of course Angela doesn't know about that though.

At some point the other day I had to stop and think to myself. Why do I care what Angela thinks? My personal life is my business. And I get to choose who I want in it. I understand that her and Venessa have a past and I'm deeply and truly sorry for that. But why should what happen to them stop me from enjoying my life? I mean, I do wish I had listened to Angela and stayed away from Venessa. But I learned my lesson, and I learned it myself.

What's life without making a few mistakes.

And speaking of mistakes. Veronica has been messaging me all day. I don't know if I'm ghosting her, nor do I know why. I just got a bad vibe from her yesterday.

I haven't read any of the texts because that would only cause my fingers to betray me and text her back.

I honestly have no logical reason for avoiding her. I like her. She seems nice and intriguing. And I know if I stop trusting everyone my life will be hell. So, like I said, what's life without a few heartbroken lessons?

All I know is that I'm enjoying myself with her now, and if things go bad in the future, that's futures me problem.

Yeah

I'm not very good with certain things.

Once I came to that conclusion I settled with myself that there's no reason to avoid her. As I was walking into my apartment I opened my phone and went to her number.

Veronica

Hey, what you doing?: 9pm yesterday

Since when do you go to sleep this early? 10:09 yesterday

I have been thinking about you all night. Please text me back: 11:15 yesterday

I woke up this morning and didn't see a notification from you and it really disappointed me. It wasn't until then that I realized I might have creeped you out the other day. I would like to sincerely apologize for that. I know I tend to come off too strong and I am utterly sorry for that. Kissing you unexpectedly like that was rude and inappropriate. I really really sorry. I would like to apologize in person. If you don't, I understand.: 9:15am this morning

I started to feel bad seeing as she thought that was the reason I was avoiding her. I mean, was that why I was avoiding her? I liked when she kissed me. Especially unexpectedly like that. But it was just that Venessa laid in the back of my head, screwing with me. And seeing as I'm done with her, I should be good.

I have decided to give up on my little mission because there's no good outcome to get to my answer.

MeMeet me at the cafe in twenty minutes.

As soon as I sent it she immediately opened it. I know that may seem wired to some people, but I like when people read my text quickly. It lets me know that I'm important enough to where they will stop doing what their doing to see what I texted.

VeronicaCan't wait to see you

A small blush creeped onto my face as I went to go take a quick shower. When I left my apartment, it was a little after 4pm and the sun was still shining brightly. I wore sunglasses that made me feel like a badass even though everyone who knows me knows I'm a gigantic pussy.

Speaking of everyone who knows me. Where the fuck is Paige?! I just realize I haven't talked to that bozo in a minute. I've been so wrapped in my own head these last few weeks that I didn't notice she has been gone.

I pulled out my phone and started walking to the cafe. I dialed her number and called her. She picked up on the fourth ring. Bitch.

"Hello?"

"And where the hell have you been?!" She snorted.

"I wondered when you were going to realize I was gone," I rolled my eyes as I crossed the street.

"I know I'm sorry. I should have realized sooner. I've just been so caught up in my life and I forgot about everyone else around me. I apologize," she started chuckling and I could just imagine her shaking her head.

"It's fine babe," I smiled.

"Well good. Where the hell are you?"

"France," I squinted my eyes. "Visiting my family. My mom got sick and everyone got scared so I came to home watch over the business. I should be back later this week though," I mentally slapped myself for not knowing she was gone. "I know your beating yourself up but I'm fine. Mom is getting better. She's yelling at everyone at the house right now no doubt. She'll be up and walking by next week,"

"Well that's good. And I wasn't beating myself up for not noticing you. I was beating myself up because I missed an opportunity to go to France," we both started laughing as I walked into the cafe.

I looked around and my smile got a little bigger once I saw Veronica. I started walking over to her. "Hey, I gotta go, but call me, ok. I miss you,"

"Will do. Love you,"

"Love you too," I hung up and sat down across Veronica. I watched as her eyes followed my phone as I sat it down on the table.

"Who was that?"

"A friend from school," she slowly nodded her head as if she didn't believe me. She cleared her throat and put her hands in her lap. It was like she was nervous. Which was weird seeing her like that. She always gave me the impression of a well put woman. I mean, I'm not saying that a strong woman can't have feelings. It's just it's hard to imagine her like that.

"Um. I know that I can off strong and like I said before, I completely apologize for that. I shouldn't have kissed you without permission. From the bottom of my heart, I am sorry," I smiled a little and nodded my head.

"I'm not mad Veronica. I didn't answer your text because I forgot to charge my phone last night. And this morning, I had just decided to leave it at home and let it charge," my smile started to go up. "and I enjoyed the kiss. Very much," her smile came back as she moved her hair back.

"Well, since that's settled, I wanted to ask you something," I nodded my head for her to continue. "I wanted to ask you if you would come up to my parents house with me this weekend? You are totally fine if you say no. I know this is a little out of the ordinary and like way too fast pace-"

"I would love to," she smiled.

"Really?" I nodded my head and this seemed to make her happy. "Oh my gosh! I thought you would say no. I can't wait for you to meet my family. Uh, a little warning. The reason why we're going is for my mom's funeral," my mouth slightly opened and my eyebrows went up.

"Oh okay," she started lightly laughing.

"Sorry to spring that up on you. It's just this is the only time my whole family will be together. And as much as I couldn't really stand my close family, I did enjoy my other relatives. Although, I can't wait for you to meet my sister," I could see the gleam in her eyes as she said that.

"I thought you and sister didn't get along," Veronica shrugged her shoulders.

"We don't. But she's always been one to brag about her life and I just can't wait to shove it in her face when she's sees the beautiful woman I have on my arm," I couldn't stop the smile that never seems to go away when I'm around her.

"I will be honored to be your arm candy," I watched as she started to bit her bottom lip making me cross my legs. This sudden arousal that keeps appearing out of nowhere is still new and unnatural for me.

"I will pick you up at 9:30 in the morning tomorrow," she said as she stood up. I followed and smiled at her. I watched as she watched me. She wanted to grab me but refrained herself.

Venessa's words played in the back up my head only making my actions more reasonable. I put my hands on Veronica's cheeks and pulled her into me. I planted my lips on to hers and her hands went to my waist.

I could feel how hungry she was by the way she kissed me. Her hands started to move down and I knew if she touched the right spot I would let her take me on this damn table in front of people, so I moved back.

She was breathing heavily and her eyes were close. "Would you like to come home with me?" She whispered. I wanted to yes. So damn bad. But I was nervous. I could sense how much she wanted to touch me but my self-conscious started to mess with me and I knew I couldn't.

"Maybe next time," I said while slowly pulling back. I didn't want her to think I was avoiding her again so I gave her a small wink before I turned around.

I had a chance to lose my virginity and I bitched out. Just my fucking luck. But I knew how much lust she had in her and I don't think I would have been able to do it. I'm not saying I want my first time to be slow and full of love but like, I don't think I can handle her like that. At least not for now.

I need to pack anyways.

****

How do y'all think this trip is gonna go? Give some good thoughts. I may just add it in there .

Trip Part 1

I can't fucking stand packing. No one, and I mean no one, knows how to do it properly. And by properly I mean having everything you need, everything packed neatly, oh, and also, being prepared and packed before the day you have to leave.

I don't think in the history of packing someone has packed everything they needed without forgetting something.

I was packed. I was ready. But I knew I was forgetting something. I just didn't know what. I was standing in the corner of my bedroom, looking over everything to see if maybe, just maybe, I can remember what it is I'm forgetting. I feel that the better question is, am I actually forgetting anything?

I think that maybe my nerves are what's causing my anxiety right now. I'm literally about to meet this woman's family.

They're probably all high class rich people with fancy attire and high paying fancy jobs like lawyers, and doctors. Why the hell would Veronica want to bring me? I don't even look smart let alone act like it.

This made me overthink my packing. Maybe I should pack something more elegant. Then they might think I'm trying too hard. I mean, I did pack one dress just in case. It is a little over the top but it's the only nice one I have.

A knock came from my door and my heart started pounding. I left my room and went to open the front door. Veronica stood there with a smile and sunglasses. "Good morning, love," I smiled too as I moved to the side. She came in and I closed the door behind me.

I watched as she looked around and I started scratching the back of my head out of nervousness. I mean I always keep my apartment clean. It's nice and tidy and homey. It's just she's probably used to mansions and penthouse and-

"I love your home," she said before I could finish my thought. She had her hands behind her back while looking over everything with a small smile.

"Thank you," I said quietly as I went back to my room and zipped up my suitcase. I stopped to check myself in the mirror. Veronica said that we are traveling by car and it's going to take up the whole day. According to her, we won't get there til about midnight. So I thought there's no point in trying to impress anyone with my outfit if everyone's going to be asleep when we get there. So I just decided on wearing some leggings and a sweatshirt. The worst feeling is wearing something uncomfortable during a long car ride.

I looked up to see Veronica smiling at me from the doorway. "It's cute," I narrowed my eyes at her in a playful manner.

"What is?" She walked towards me and wrapped her arms around my waist while looking at me through the mirror.

"How scared you are," I chuckled softly and she kissed my cheek. "You're going to be fine. My family may be an ass to me but when it comes to the outside world, they are as perfect as can be," I snorted.

"So they're fake,"

"Absolutely," I groaned, causing her to laugh. She turned me around to face her and held the sides of my face. "It's going to be alright. I promise. And besides," she put her hands back around my waist and brought me closer into her. "I'll be right next to you the entire time," I looked up at her.

"Promise?" she smiled and nodded. She leaned down and planted her lips on mine. I've gotten used to her kissing me and I really enjoy it. Her hands started to move down to my ass as she slowly walked me backwards. She laid me down on the bed without breaking the kiss. Her lips went down to my neck and a moan passed my lips. It wasn't until that certain shock went through my body, that I realized for some reason, I felt guilt lay inside of me.

I swallowed the lump in the back of my throat and forced a laugh. "I think we should get going," she hummed in response and kissed down my neck. Her hands started traveling up my sweatshirt and her cold hands made me flinch.

"We have more than enough time," she whispered. When I felt her hand at the hem of my bra my brain started to panic.

"Come on, I'm dying to meet these people you have so much hatred for," I said through a forced tone of joy. I somehow flipped her over to where I was sitting on top of her. She looked me over while biting her bottom lip and sighed.

"Fine. But we will be finishing this tonight," I nodded with a smile and she rolled me back over and deeply kissed me. If it wasn't for me pulling away with a smile, she would have kept going.

I watched as she picked up my suitcase and looked at me. "You got everything?" I looked around my room, knowing damn well I'm forgetting something.

"I guess so. Let's go,"

******

Before we started to leave the state, Veronica told me she had to stop by her sister's business to make sure she's heading out. When she got out of the car, it dawned to me that her sister lives here. And she has her own fucking building! Which just adds to the excitement of meeting her rich and important family. I mean, I don't just want to call her rich, no doubt she probably is, but more of she's successful. If she's anything like Veronica, she most definitely made a name for herself, by herself. And I mean no shit, I knew her sister lived here, it just didn't occur to me that you know. Hell I don't even know. My brain doesn't process things right.

Whenever I had looked around to see where we were at, I didn't really see anything. There were a few restaurants every here and there, but Veronica didn't walk towards any of them. This area does seem vaguely familiar, but I do know I've never been over here.

When she got back in the car I finally decided to ask the question that I should have asked before I even agreed to go with her. "So, where are we going?" I watched as she smiled and started her car. I had made myself some hot cocoa before I left the house.

"California," and I damn near spit it out when she said that. I looked at her wide-eyed.

"I'm pretty sure that's going to take more than a few hours,"

"40, to be exact," I didn't say anything but instead bit my bottom lip and slowly nodded my head. She started laughing and put her hand on my thigh. "Don't worry, love. It's just going to be you, me, and the road. Plus, we'll have plenty of time to get to know one another," I didn't know what to say so I just smiled and agreed with her.

Truth be told, I can't stand to be in a small confined space with any for more than six hours. The last time I went on a trip with some of my close friends back home, I wanted to rip their throats out after two days of being in a hotel with them. Now, imagine what 40 hours in a car with one person is going to be like.

As she started driving, I emailed all my professors to send me the work we're going to be doing on Monday and Tuesday. It's Saturday morning at the moment so hopefully I'll be back within five days.

******

There's literally no point in prolonging the entire trip. I doubt any of you want to sit there and listen to how an entire 40 hours of a car ride went. Grant it, I did last longer than six hours before I started to get annoyed. Honestly, it wasn't that bad. When the sun started to leave us, we had stopped at a hotel.

We shared a bed and I could just feel and sense how much she wanted to touch me. And I wanted to do the same. But I couldn't.

There was this feeling in my stomach that started to ache everytime I even thought about being physical with her.

She didn't seem to mind though, and I thank her for that. I do think she could sense that I was somehow avoiding her. That night whenever she climbed on top of me, I used the excuse that I was tired. I thought that would be a good excuse seeing as I stayed up with her the entire ride to talk to her.

The next morning though, I could see how frustrated she was. Maybe she woke up on the wrong side, or she wasn't looking forward to the drive. Either way, I could see how upset she was.

One thing I have always hated about myself is how I would go lengths to make someone feel better. Even if it comes at my own expense.

So when I tell you that I had asked Veronica to join me in the shower that morning, I didn't really want her in there with me. But when I saw her smile I knew I had made her feel better.

She got into the shower with me, I was facing away from her. I could feel her eyes on me and all I wanted to do was shrink into the drain. I slightly jumped when I felt her arms wrap around my waist.

Her front was pressed up against my back and her nose was buried between my neck. She started to slowly kiss my neck and I sighed in content once I felt her bite down. It wasn't until I felt her tongue against my skin that the memory came back.

A small moan slipped my mouth as I could feel her hands against my stomach, her lips on my skin, her breast touching my back. Her breathing tickled me making a small smile form on my lips. But it was when she bit my ear that realization hit.

I was thinking about Venessa the entire time.

Guilt filled me as her hands started to move down between my legs. "I'm not ready," the words pushed out my mouth before I could comprehend what they were. She paused for a second then removed herself from me. "I'm sorry," I said just above a whisper. Guilt filling my insides.

"There's nothing to be sorry about, love. When you're ready, I'll be right here," I started to turn around to face her but she stopped me. "If you turn around I won't be able to stop myself," she kissed my cheek. "Come on, let's hurry up. We still have a long way to go,"

That was really the only simi-awkward moment of the trip. We didn't really talk the rest of the way, except some small talk every here and there and when we stopped to get something to eat.

It wasn't a bad silence, but it wasn't good either. She did seem to be in a better mood than she was this morning so I guess that's good.

About time we made it to her family's house it was one in the morning. I helped her carry some stuff in and I couldn't help but be at awe, but also feel intimidated, at how beautiful the house was.

It was fucking huge.

I didn't really have the energy in me though to say anything because I was too tired. Veronica noticed and decided to be overdramatic and carried me upstairs. I couldn't help but giggle the entire way, making her laugh.

She laid me down on a bed and tucked me in. "You coming," I asked as she started to walk away.

"Yeah, I'm just going to go get our stuff. But you get some sleep," she came back over to me and kissed my forehead. "Tomorrow is going to be one hell of a day,"

Trip Part 2

Just watched 'Marry Me' with Jennifer Lopez. Go watch it. It was so good.

******

I felt hands on my body. Love surrounded me in every direction. I wanted her to touch me but the words couldn't form in my mouth. But they didn't have to. She knew what I wanted and how I wanted it. She knew everything. Her back was pressed up against my front. Her lips were grazing against the skin of my neck. I threw my head back against her shoulder as she started chuckling in my ear. Her laugh is what brought a smile to my face. It was so genuine. So enchanting. The emotions and feeling running through my body wasn't just desire. It was longing. Aching. Dare I might say love. With her arms wrapped around me so tightly I felt safe. I have never felt this safe in anyone's arms. But shes manged to break down my walls.

Her lips moved down my neck leaving marks everywhere she touched. I couldn't stop the smile that seemed to have a permanent residency on my face. And I didn't mind it one bit. She started laughing again. Ugh, her laugh makes my heart flutter everytime.

I woke up today with the feeling of someone staring at me. Has that every happened to you? Whether your sleeping or awake, you just feel a certain presence near you or looking at you? It's annoying and irritating.

When I opened my eyes the first thing I saw was Veronica smiling at me. My anger went away, not completely, and I smiled at her. "Good morning," she said with a faint smile on her face. I hummed in response as I turned my face against the pillow, hoping to suffocate myself.

I didn't sleep very well through the night. These dreams came to me every time I closed my eyes. I woke up at least twice, a wetness between my legs. Fear scourge through me as I thought I wet myself. But it didn't smell like it. I had looked it up on my phone and according to google, I had something called a wet dream.

I could stop from blushing to myself. The dreams that I had were very lust filled and exciting. And that's weird considering I don't really ever remember my dreams.

I didn't really doubt much of this though, but I also didn't fully believe it. I asked Google about a cough I had and it told me I had cancer. So I'm a little skeptical.

"Come on. Every is awake, people are starting to arrive," at this, my head shot up. Realization of where I was, who I was with, why I was here, it all hit me at one time. I sat up fully and covered my mouth with my hands.

"Oh God, oh God! I'm going to be late. Ugh! What a terrible first impression I'm going to make!" I covered my face completely and I soon felt arms wrap around me.

"It's okay, love," Veronica said with a small chuckle at the end. "Remember what I told you. Everyone here is fake and a bunch of assholes. Do not worry about them. And hey!" She pulled my hands away from my face. "The later the better. It's always best to make a grand entrance," I rolled my eyes at her and slapped her shoulder. She laughed and grabbed my hands.

There was something familiar in her laugh. But it wasn't an exact.

She pulled me into her and planted a slow and tender kiss upon my lips. "You're going to do great. You have absolutely nothing to worry about," I took a deep breath as I repeated her words in my head and nodded.

"Ok, I got this,"

"You got this,"

"Ok. I'm going to go take a shower then get dress. I need about an hour," she smiled widely. But there was something in her eyes that caught my attention. A look I knew well too much.

Mischief.

I watched as she walked away and out the room. Giving me privacy to get ready. And so I did.

I took about ten minutes in the shower, fifteen doing my hair, twenty to do my make-up, and the rest of the time consisted of me finding the right outfit.

I wanted to wear the dress that I had brought but decided against it. Even if everyone downstairs is all dressed up fancy, I'll just stick out. I rather that to happen then me going down there looking like a whore and every is wearing family Christmas sweaters.

I tucked my red silk shirt into my white jeans and put on a pair of red heels. They show style, class, and power. I learned that from a certain someone during one of our sessions.

I put on some jewelry. Not too much but enough to heighten my appearance.

I looked in the mirror one last time. What is the literal worst that could happen? I always find myself asking that everytime I'm afraid. The worst that could happen to me is that I die. And considering there is a very low chance of that happening to me today, I should be fine.

I fasten my belt while putting my phone in my back pocket and walked out the room.

I forgot how grand this house was, so imagine how stunned and lost I looked. With every step I took I couldn't help but stop and just take in my surroundings.

I heard noise coming so I followed it all the way to downstairs.

I stood at the stop of the staircase and looked down. There had to be about thirty people here. They were all spread out, considering how big the house was.

As I was walking down the stairs, I caught a few eyes. I tired not to pay much attention to them, but that still didn't stop the overwhelming anxiety coursing through my veins. I did so happen though to glance at everyone's outfits.

They were all in bougie tan sweaters and white or faded pants.

It made me stand it out.

And somewhere deep down, I liked it. I liked having the attention. I liked how people stopped to stare at me. I liked how my back straightened, how I rose my head, how I walked down those stairs, feeling power in every step. My red shirt is what grabbed the attention is what I like to think.

A quick history lesson. During a wedding, if a woman in the audience wore red, it was a statement that she had slept with the groom.

I shuffled around people as I could feel the small ounce of confidence I had in me drain away.

I soon found Veronica and her eyes grazed over me. "You look amazing, mon amour," she said in a full thick French accent. I couldn't help but smile as she wrapped her arms around my waist. "Come one," she started guiding me back to the stairs, where we stopped a third of the way.

She tapped her wine glass with a spoon, to which I didn't even notice she had in her hand.

I started to shrink down a little as everyone turned to face us. "I would like to introduce you all to someone very special to me," she moved over a little and everyone looked at me.

It was weird. I've never had so much attention before. But as I watched as men stared me over, and woman talked amongst themselves, no doubt pin pointing everything wrong about me, it was the mere fact that it was I who was the center of attention. And from that moment on, I knew, I had craved this.

The attention.

I looked over at Veronica with a smile hoping to receive one back. But she wasn't looking at me. She was looking straight a head

I followed her line of sight to see the last person I would expect. But she wasn't looking back at Veronica. She was looking at me. Staring at me. Her eyes held something. Anger. Hatred. But it wasn't for me.

And that's when I realized. I've been pawn in a game of chess that I didn't even know was going on.

"Oh Dr. Morgan. Why must you bring so much pain to me?" I whispered to myself.

Trip Part 3

Dr. Morgan's POV.

I hate everyone here.

Every face I see. Every hand that touches me. Every eye that looks my way, I want to punch to the fucking ground. They're all judging me, that I know. They've done it my entire life, and thankfully I learned at an early age how to ignore them.

During my ride down here I knew there was no way in hell I was going to survive in this house for four days by myself. So I called a friend, the only friend, I had during high school. She had moved down here during 9th grade but left after the year was over with.

I'd only had been friends with her for a short period of time, but during that time, she felt more like family to me than any other person.

Aaron had found her, thank god, and I had contacted her, unfortunately, I don't know if she got it or not.

I looked around at everyone. Assholes. They were all wealthy, selfish, jackasses. Makes me fit right in. I'm wealthy, selfish, and a gigantic jackass. You would think I would love these people. That

I would take humility in them. But I don't like people like me. I'm better than them. Not in every aspect, but better than them.

I sipped my glass of wine in the corner at the back of the room. I grew up in this house. I know every hall, every secret passageway, everything. I couldn't help but smile as I remembered Veronica and me as kids, running around, playing tag. The small moments that never lasted.

I saw movement and a flash of red cross my eyes. I looked up to see a woman. I couldn't keep my eyes off her. Something about her drew me into her. Maybe it was just the fact that she stood out above the rest.

Or maybe it was because she wore the face of the one person who has been upholding my mind for the past month.

My mouth dropped a little as she looked over the crowd from above. There was fear in her eyes. Doubt. But as she continued to watch, her attitude changed. I watched as she descended down the stairs. Confidence building with every step.

Her shoulders were slender back as she straightened herself up. She put her chin up, she looked forward, not paying attention to anyone around her. Pairs of eyes looked dead at her as she continued to walk. The mumors around me got louder as they all talked about her. Although my mind was confused, a part of me was impressed. Proud even.

She held her head up high. She stood her ground.

But as she got off the stairs I could see that light in her die down. I moved away from the wall I was leaning on and followed her from a distance.

I watched as her hips swayed with every step she took.

Someone stopped me in my tracks causing me to lose her. I glared at the man in front of me. I remember him. He hated me. I don't know why though. Maybe it was because my dick was bigger than his. Or maybe because I slept with his wife.

And sister.

And his daughter.

We're not related by the way.

Before he could say anything I turned and walked away. I couldn't find her now, which is weird considering she outstands everyone here.

My head snapped up as I heard a glass being tapped. "I would like to introduce you all to someone very special to me," I rolled my eyes. The sound of her voice infuriated me. But my curiosity took over as I looked at my sister. There was someone standing behind her.

And it wasn't until I saw that flash of red that made my eyes go round. "No," I whispered to myself.

As everyone turned their eyes to Veronica and Olivia, Veronica found my eyes, and I watched as a giant grin appeared on her face.

I looked at Olivia as she smiled. She was happy. I could tell how much she loved the unwanted attention. She turned to look at Veronica expecting her to be looking at her as well. She followed Veronica's eye view. Soon, we were looking at one another.

I watched as that bright light in her eyes slowly disappeared. Anger scourged through me as Veronica continued to grin at me. But what made me furious was when I saw everything in Olivia die. She figured out what has happened. She figured out why it happened.

I bawled my hands into a fist as I imagined running it into Veronica's face.

Olivia looked at Veronica with anger and tears in her eyes. Veronica looked down at Olivia with a smile filled with pity. She tried to comfort her, no doubt telling her that it was only a unfortunate coincidence. Olivia shook her head and speed-walked down the stairs and out the house through the back door.

I knew Veronica wanted to make me jealous, so I played her game. I held the angry stare at her so she wouldn't go after Olivia. She walked away slowly while still grinning at me.

Once she was out of view I quickly walked outside. I shut the screen door behind me and looked to my right to see her sitting on the bench that faced the water fountain.

I approached her from behind and quietly sat down next to her.

I watched as a single tear rolled down her cheek, but I reframed myself from wiping it. "This used to be my favorite place to come when I was younger," she quickly wiped her face. "When I felt sad, or felt like an outcast. Or when I felt like giving up. My life that is," I sighed as I watched the water. The way it flowed so freely. Or at least that's what it wanted you to think. It was actually controlled by a filter. Everyone knew it but never says anything. Because we look at what we see. We don't think about the story behind it.

"I watched you walk down the stairs you know," I slightly chuckled. "The way you held yourself up. You didn't care what anyone said. You knew the way you looked and you didn't need anyone's approval. And I hate to say it, but there were people talking about you. Good and bad. But the bad was mere jealousy," I heard her scuff and I rolled my eyes. I sighed and crossed my legs. "During the 1500's era, back when they had kings and queens and beheadings and shit, before tv was invented or internet, or anything that keeps our modern day world entertained. Women didn't really have a roll in life but to carry a child. Some men even referred to them as not a person but merely a vessel. So what did these women do to pass their time? They talked about people. They would gossip to one another about someone else. If a woman from out of town came in wearing something that didn't fit their style, these women talked behind their back. But the only reason they did that, was because they had nothing better to do.

Their lives were so fucking miserable, they tortured other women with their words. And I hate to tell you, but modern women haven't changed. Our roles in society might have. We might have gotten stronger, and fierce, and political. But others, they do what their ancestors did," I gently grabbed her by her chin and made her look at me. "Don't let the words of others effect your way of life. Don't take the advice of someone who has not walked your path. You are your own person. You have the world in the palm of your hands. Take advantage of it. Don't think about anyone else but you," I was looking directly into those brown eyes I have come to adore so much.

I could see that my words were getting to her, but it quickly vanished as she started to think.

"Is that what you say to all your patients to get them into your bed?" The betrayal in her eyes were on the surface and I hated it.

"I have never taken anyone to my bed. I don't usually give history lessons. And I don't encourage them this much. I usually tell them how worthless they are and that they need to do better. They ask how to do that. And then from there, there are multiple roads to take. But every single one of them leads to the same destination," she pulled her chin from my hand and stood up. "Did you expect me not to tell the truth? I wouldn't lie to you, Olivia. Even if the truth hurts-"

"You lied to me about having a sister!"

"I don't have a sister," she scuffed and started to walk away. "That woman in there," she stopped. "That woman you were with. Is not. My sister. We may share the same blood and the same last name, but she is dead to me," she turned to look at me. "She may play the goodie-too-shoes who loves everyone, and wants to be friends with everyone, and encourages you when you have no faith in yourself. But here's the thing. She's not," I walked towards her until I was standing right in front of her.

"She dates people. She brings them home to meet the family so that that person feels special. She tells them how much she cares about them and how beautiful they are. She sleeps with them and makes love to them. She makes that person feel loved. But after a month or so. She leaves. Without a word. Without a hint of a reason why. Because the truth is, she doesn't care about anyone around her except herself. She doesn't love anyone except herself. She tells these people how amazing they are so they'll depend on her. But you don't need reassurance. Because you know your worth. Or at least you need to,"

More tears were streaming from her eyes, but this time I didn't restrain myself from wiping them. "You will never have to beg the right person to love you. And if I'm being honest," I lifted up her chin with my fingers. "I really hope you don't love her," She looked up at me.

"Why?" She asked quietly. I couldn't figure out the answer, but I knew it. But there was no way in hell the words would come out my mouth. Because I care about you. I thought. But couldn't say. I watched as she shook her head and stepped away from me. "I don't know what your playing at. But I'm done. With you and your entire fucked up family," she walked away from me and back inside. I wanted to call after but my voice wouldn't let me.

"That was fucking pathetic," my head snapped to my right to see someone leaning against a tree with a glass of wine in their hand. "But from what I heard, not that I was snooping or anything, which I was by the way," I rolled my eyes. "We need to get rid of your sister. And I believe we are both completely capable of doing so. Me more than you obviously," I crossed my arms and slightly smiled.

"Well, if it isn't the infamous Scarlett Rose. To what do I owe this pleasure," she pushed herself off the tree.

"You fucking invited me," I shrugged.

"Didn't think you'd come," she hummed in response as she walked towards me.

"Considering you sent me an email instead of a text, neither did I. Who the fuck emails?" I couldn't stop myself from laughing even if I wanted to. This woman has been the only person to ever make me genuinely laugh. "Now, back to what I said. Your sister. I think she needs to go,"

******What could possibly go wrong now??

Trip Part 4

Dr. Morgan's POV

"I could kill her you know,"

"Why is that always your first fucking thought?!"

"You got a better idea?!"

"How about one that doesn't involve me murdering my sister?!"

"I didn't say you had to do it,"

"Don't you have a kid on the way? I doubt your wife or other kids would like to see their mother in prison," Scarlett shrugged her shoulders.

"Please, like a cell could hold me. I would be out of there is less than a week. I have hotels, cabins, fucking mansions all over this planet. And that's even if it came to that. A judge wouldn't convict me," I crossed my arms and leaned back.

"And what makes you so sure of that?" I watched as she smirked while taking a drink of her wine.

"Out of my fifteen years of being P.A, you really think I've never been to court?" I squinted my eyes and she chuckled. "I'm good V.

But not that good. Grant it, I always find my way out of getting convicted,"

"Well you have to be good enough to get out of a murder charge," she nodded her head.

"Fair enough," Everyone was here now. Family and friends. Old and new. I recognized some faces, most I didn't know. I always hated family reunions especially as a child. As a child, you are known by whoever your parents are.

I haven't seen Olivia since she went back inside which was about twenty minutes ago. I didn't want to go look for her in fear that she left. I wouldn't be surprised though if she did. Veronica is still here, talking to people, making them laugh.

Bitch.

Why the fuck is she talking to other people when she should be confronting Olivia. She lied to her for this long, the least she can do is continue the lie. This isn't like Veronica though. When she takes someone to a family event, she shows them off for as long as she can. She showed Olivia off and threw her to the side as if she did her part and was now useless.

This caused my anger to boil. Veronica played her as if it was nothing. She wanted to make me jealous, she wanted my attention. She wanted to make a statement that she was better than me. She used Olivia for her own personal gain. But I had to stop and think though because I realized...that's exactly what I do. That's exactly what I was doing to her. And not once did I stop to think about the emotional toll it took on her.

"I don't want her to die," I said to Scarlett as I was staring at Veronica from across the room. She seemed happy. Joyful. As if her life was complete. "I want her to suffer. I want her to know what it's like to have everything taken from you at the last moment, right when you think you have the world in you grasps, it gets snatched away," I watched as Scarlett hummed in satisfaction.

"God I miss this," I turned my head to face her in questioning. "After I got married and had kids, I decided to put down my knives," my mouth slightly gaped open. "It was time. I only ever did those things because I had a empty space in my chest. When I met Vivian," I watched as a smile crept on to her lips as she looked at her feet. "That woman gave me everything I have ever dreamt of and more. There was no need for me to continue my work," I watched as she gulped down the rest of her drink. "So I killed Simon then left,"

I would say I was surprised but I wasn't. "Ah yes, Simon. I never liked him. We stopped talking to one another after you two got in bed together,"

"Please don't fucking use that term," I laughed and slapped her shoulder.

"Hey, you remember that little girl that always used to follow you around? She was so precious," Scarlett nodded her head with a smile.

"Yeah, Harper. We actually just got back in touch not to long ago. She's married now. Three kids," I hummed in response. Out of the three of us, I never thought Scarlett would be the one to settle down.

When I was younger, I never thought I would meet other girls like me. But I did. That's mainly why Scarlett and I became friends. She helped me build up my confidence. And I couldn't thank her enough for that. "Imagine if we all stuck together,"

"Three bitches with a dick. Ugh, we would be unstoppable," Scarlett said and I agreed. "But Harper was always too much of a softie. She had a big heart. Still does," I hummed in response. Before I could say anything more I saw something move in the corner of my eye.

I watched as someone closed the door to the bathroom. But before it closed I saw a flash of red. I stood up and turned to Scarlett. "Watch Veronica,"

"If she comes up to me I will stab a fork into her neck and watch her bleed out on to this damn floor,"......how the fuck am I supposed to respond to that? Instead, I just shook my head and walked away. I would really like to believe she was joking but I know damn well she's not.

I walked up the stairs and slightly opened up the door. In the mirror I could see her taking off her shirt. My eyes couldn't take themselves off her body. I swallowed the lump in my throat and looked down at my feet. For the first time in my life, I felt somewhat bad for looking at someone without them knowing.

I cleared my throat and quietly knocked on the door. She slightly jumped and looked at me. Once we made eye contact she rolled her eyes. I stepped in while still not looking at her and closed the door behind me.

After a few seconds I looked up to see her putting on a tan sweater that seemingly went with everyone else's. I sighed a little out of sorrow and frustration. "I told you, there's no need for you to fit in with these people, Miss Wilson," she scoffed.

"So we're back to Miss Wilson now?" She tucked her shirt into her pants then bent down to pick up her other shirt. My eyes immediately went to her ass.

Once she stood up and caught me, I didn't bother looking away.

I went to go sit down on the bathtub and just stared at her. The gleam and light and joy that was in her eyes only an hour ago was gone. I've never seen her look like this. And yet. She still looked perfect in every way. If only she could see it. "You don't need me to tell you how beautiful you are. Cause you already know that," it wasn't until a look of doubt crossed her that I realized, I keep thinking she's somewhere she's not.

I looked down at my hands and sighed. I stood up and slowly walked towards her. "But. If I wanted to be cocky. And I wanted to act like a man who believes a woman needed my reassurance to feel special" she slightly chuckled. "I would tell you that you are the most kindest, gorgeous, talented woman I have ever met. You don't cry in front of anyone, you hold your ground, you don't let anyone see you fault. And for those exact reason. You have my respect. And not many people do," we were staring at one another now.

"Is that supposed to make me feel better?" She knew what I said was right but didn't want to listen, to me at least. She's stubborn. And fighter.

I guess I must have been gazing at her for too long because she looked away and shook her head. "I don't know why I ever believed her. You. I saw the red flags but chose to ignore them because I felt alive, happy," she chuckled and continued to shake her head. "Maybe my mother was right. I'm nothing more than a mistake," I watched as her eyes became watery and my therapist mind took over. Her parents.

She just shook her head and wiped her face. "Uh, as painful as this was. I'm glad I got to know you Venessa," words wanted to come out my mouth but they wouldn't. I wanted to hold her. But I couldn't. It's not in my nature to care. And yet, here I am. She gave me one last look before she walked away.

"Victoria," the word came out before I could process it. She stopped walking and turned to look back at me. "Victoria Morgan. That's my name,"

Trip Part 5

Sorry this took so long. I'll give you two.

****

Victoria. Why didn't I think of that? I mean, I'm so used to calling her Venessa it kind of just stuck with me. But Victoria. That just fits her perfectly. It's elegant. Perfect. But it's not that. It's the fact that she told me.

I mean, that shouldn't really mean anything. Should it? She's never told anyone, or so she says. She's lied to me before, what's stopping her from doing it now? I am so damn gullible. A pretty woman, with a pretty face, with a sense of authority, she's composed, she knows what she wants and she takes it. How could I not fall for it? Clearly many people have.

And while we're on the topic, she has slept with countless people as far as I know. She's experienced in every way...hold up...why am I thinking about that? She's...I don't...nothing. She has a penis.

That thought immediately came to mind causing me to choke on my water.

I never really thought about it seeing as I didn't really see her that way, or at least not that much. I was sitting in the back of the living room with a glass of water. I'm not really much of an alcohol drinker, plus I would like to stay sober for the time being. Everyone was still talking to one another. I do think that we're about to start.

Although, I'm pretty sure the funeral won't begin till tomorrow. Why the hell am I here again? Oh yeah, a very hot woman lured me here to brag to her sister who just so happens to also be hot. And my therapist.

But out of everything that has happened, the only question that lingered in my head was, did Veronica actually like me, or was she just using me?

The emotions and feelings that were running through my veins about Venessa-well Victoria, telling me her name, over clouded the hurt and pain I was feeling from Veronica.

I felt someone staring at me making me look around. I had changed my shirt, hoping to stop the eyes from following me.

My eyes stopped one I found the source. Veronica was staring at me from across the room. I couldn't really read the look on her face but nevertheless, I didn't want her looking at me. The only reason why I'm still here is because I don't have a ride home. And I don't have the money on me for a plane ticket.

I got up out of my seat and started walking around. The sun was at its highest making it hot as hell. I wanted it to be night, then I could just go to lay down. I like to procrastinate by sleeping.

Apparently that's called depression.

I tried to avoid being seen. I wasn't exactly in the mood to talk to anyone. I doubt anyone would come up to me though. These people probably haven't seen one another in ages. None of them would even bother to look at me twice now that I blend in.

I made my way outside, in the back, where there were fewer people. I wonder what their parents do. Probably retired surgeons or something. Maybe their a doctor family and Victoria took a different route. I mean, she's still a doctor of some sort.

Speaking of. My eyes found her and she was standing next to a woman. A very tall, dominant woman. I didn't think it was possible to see someone more fearsome than Victoria, but hell.

The woman said something causing both her and Victoria to laugh. Something inside me lit up as I watched them. I've never seen her laugh like that. Genuinely laugh. I don't know whether it was because I've never seen her laugh like that or if it was a touch of jealousy that struck down on me. Either way, I didn't like it.

Something took over me as I walked over to them. My brain was screaming stop and turn away, but my feet weren't listening. I knew whatever was about to happen was going to be embarrassing at the end but to hell with it.

As soon as I was near her, as if my brain couldn't be more stupid, I wrapped my arms around her waist and buried my nose into her shoulder.

She slightly stiffened until she looked down at me. It was quiet for a second giving me enough time to realize what I'm doing. What the fuck and I doing?!!

That doubt subsided though once I felt her arm wrap around my shoulder. A small smile formed on my lips as she took the glass of water out of my hand. "How come you're not drinking?" She asked as she sat my glass down on the table.

I shrugged my shoulders. "I'm tired," she hummed in response as if she knew I was lying.

"Vivian does this when she doesn't want me talking to someone. It's cute when they get jealous," the woman said.

"I'm not jealous. There's no need to be jealous," I said in a snarky tone as I looked at the woman. Immediately though I backed down as she stared me down. I could see she was a woman of power, anger even. That anger has subsided though. But it was still there.

"You're right. V isn't interested in women like me," the woman looked me up and down with a grin. "She's interested in pathetic little girls who can't say speak up for themselves,"

I pushed away from Victoria. "Excuse me," the woman started to slightly chuckle.

"Well hell, you might have a little fire in you," she looked me over once more. "Or have you had enough sessions with Dr. Morgan?-"

"You know what-" I started to leap towards the woman but Victoria grabbed my wrist.

"I think that's enough for today. Scarlett, I would appreciate if you would stop playing your mind games for five fucking seconds," the woman, Scarlett, shrugged her shoulders with a smile.

"How else am I supposed to get to know her? You only truly know a person once you see them angry," I have no doubt, veins were popping out of my head. My blood was boiling and I wanted to knock the shit out of this woman.

"I will see you tomorrow. I really do appreciate you coming though. I've missed seeing you," Scarlett nodded her head. Victoria let go of my wrist and embraced her into a hug. I was glaring at both of them the entire time. Once they pulled back, Scarlett smirked and winked at me then walked away. "She is happily married with two kids and another on the way-"

"And why do I get the feeling she wouldn't be the first woman you slept with who was married," I said without looking at her. She lightly sighed in response because she knew I was right.

"I've never slept with her. She's not my type-"

"And I am?" I turned to look at her. I know she stutters on her words in her head but I couldn't care less at the moment. "Am I your type? Helpless, needy, pathetic? Because if that's what you think of me-"

"I don't-"

"Then what the fuck do you want from me?!" I could sense people turn their heads to look at us but I didn't care. I watched as she swallowed the lump in the back of her throat and looked around.

"Can we please not do this here?" she whispered as she continued to look everywhere but at me.

"Why are you like this?" I asked. After a few seconds she finally looked down at me. "Everywhere I go, people tell me how terrible you are. How heartless and cruel, and just a bitch you are in every spectrum. But when I'm around, your not like that. I can see, right now, how scared you are. And maybe it's just me. Maybe I see more to you than others. And I know I sound like a fucking pick me girl right now, but, why are you like this with me?"

She didn't say anything. She didn't respond. And she didn't want to. She wasn't thinking about it. Nor was she debating with herself if she should answer. Because she already knew the answer.

"Because that's just the way she is," I turned around to see Veronica standing there with her arms crossed, staring at Victoria. "She doesn't care for anyone but herself, and I don't know how many times I have to tell you that Olivia," she turned her head to look at me. "I hurt you, and I take full responsibility for that. I won't stand here and lie and say that I'm sorry for what I did because I already had my intentions set from the moment I saw you walk out of her office. But I am sorry that I hurt you. You didn't deserve that. You are a very charismatic and intelligent young woman and I applaud you for that. But you're gullible. You want someone to love you so bad that you fall into a trap that you personally watched be set up. And if it wasn't for that-"

Before she could even finish her sentence, Victoria grabbed her by her shirt and punched her dead in the face.

A gasp left everyone's mouth, including mine, as Veronica fell to the ground.

Victoria got on top of her and started punching her. Every time Victoria's fist clashed with Veronica's face someone gasped.

I stood there in shock not knowing what to do. About six different people ran towards them, trying to pull Victoria up but she wouldn't budge.

It wasn't until I started seeing blood that my brain snapped into place.

They finally pulled Victoria off Veronica but she was still fighting against them. Two people helped Veronica off the ground and she had blood all over her face.

Victoria elbowed someone in the nose causing them to let go of her, which was enough to set herself free from everyone else's grip. She started to charge towards Veronica again. "Victoria stop!" I yelled as I grabbed her arm. I understand being pissed at someone and punching them. But by the look in her eyes, she wanted to kill her sister. "You need to stop. This has gone too far," I gritted through my teeth as I put my hand on her chest, as if I could actually stop her from hurting Veronica any more. "You've done enough," her eyes were still fixated on Veronica. I grabbed her chin and made her look at me. "Vic. Let's go,"

My words seemed to have an effect on her as her breathing started to slow. She scoffed and started to angrily chuckle as she turned and walked away. "You told her your name?" Veronica said. Vic turned back around to look at Veronica. Everyone was now looking between the three of us.

Victoria and Veronica seemed to have some type of nonverbal communication as Veronica's eyes got big. "Oh," was all she said.

I looked over at Vic as she looked at me.

And it was at that moment that I realized that all these mixed feelings I've been having towards her, and how she's constantly been on my mind. It wasn't all one sided.

Miss Wilson

I watched as she paced back and forth. I could tell she was pissed, anyone could. She just beat the hell out of her sister. But the anger that she put into those punches wasn't just anger that came from nowhere. It was built up anger and frustration. All those years she spent with Veronica and her family, all of it came out.

Everyone was still outside helping Veronica. They also knew not the bother Victoria right now.

After a few minutes of her pacing, she stopped to look out the window. I could tell she was deep in thought and didn't want to bother her. But sitting here in silence was getting to me. "I had always wondered as a kid if my life, my family, would be better if we had money," I started saying as I got onto the bed and leaned back against the headboard.

We were in her old room, dark and mysterious as I call it.

"I pondered with myself that if we were able to go on family trips, and picnics, and festivals, then maybe we would have been happy. My mother could never forget nor forgive what my father did to her, and neither could I. I still can't," I started chuckling. "But I never ceased to stop myself from daydreaming. That if I just had money, my life would be so much better,"

"Money doesn't solve your problems," I nodded my head with a heartbroken smile.

"Yeah. I somewhat noticed that today," she grunted as if it was supposed to be a laugh but held it in. "Veronica had told me one day, that uh, you always seemed to be the black sheep of the family. That you didn't just drift away, you were simply never with them, to begin with," she was still staring out the window with her arms crossed.

"I was never meant for this family. We share similar traits, but in the end, I'm nothing like them. And they're nothing like me," this time she did chuckle. "They never wanted me Olivia. I was their greatest and biggest mistake. But not even a year later when my mother was pregnant with Veronica, they were more than happy to welcome her in with open arms," she shook her head as she looked down at her feet.

She was crying on the inside whether she wanted to admit it or not.

I sighed as I looked at her. I'm not really one to comfort someone, especially if that someone has a Ph.D. in areas that revolve around helping people. "How about we get a hotel and stay there for the night?"

"Better yet. I just leave now," she didn't give me time to object before she grabbed her suitcase from under her bed and started walking towards the door. I guess she knew she wasn't going to stay because she didn't bother to unpack.

"Or!" I said as I stepped in front of her. "We get a fucking hotel and clear our heads," she looked at me.

"We?" I rolled my eyes.

"Would you rather have me stay here with your sister? Because I've been told once or twice that I'm very gullible. And if that's so true, who knows, I might just forgive Veronica for what she did. And if I forgive her enough," I raised my left eyebrow up and squinted my eyes with a devilish look.

She glared at me and I just grinned.

******

I ran the rag over her knuckles. She was trying hard to not flench back but I could see it was hurting her. I couldn't help but chuckle to myself seeing as she's trying to act as if she's invincible.

I could sense her eyes on me since we sat down, and I honestly don't mind. I've come to realize that it's what she does when she doesn't know what to say. She wants to understand me first before she says something. And although that's frustrating, I understand.

Blood kept running from her knuckles every time I moved the rag away making me irritated. "Why won't you stop bleeding?" I asked, mainly to myself as I dipped the rag in hot water then reapplied it to her hand.

"Because it's stubborn," she said as she continued to stare at me. I sighed deeply as I moved my hair out of my face. I didn't know how I was feeling, and I didn't want to know. I guess she and I share that. Silence filled the hotel room as it has for the past fifteen minutes. Once we got here her hand looked like it was on the edge of an infection. She didn't pay much attention to it but I couldn't stop staring at it.

Plus if she did get an infection I wouldn't be able to forgive myself. Although, I would sleep better knowing that she was too stubborn to take care of it herself. She wouldn't let me help at first, but one thing I have learned is that if you do what you want without asking, people can't really tell you no because you're already doing it.

So I grabbed a cup and filled it with hot water and a rag. She was already sitting on the bed, so I went up to her and started cleaning it. She didn't refuse or say anything so I just kept going. "So," I said with a small smile. "Victoria," she rolled her eyes making me smile. "What? How come you don't like it? It's a very elegant name. Victoria Morgan. I like it,"

"Well I don't," she responded in a flat tone. I stopped cleaning her hand once I noticed no more blood was coming out. I looked up at her and tilted.

"Do you not like it because it sounds stupid, or because it was the name your parents gave you?" She looked at me surprised. Not expecting me to actually ask a deep and meaningful question. She didn't bother answering me though. "I'm starting to accept that your silence means you're agreeing with me," I stood up and grabbed a few bandages from the first aid kit.

"Aren't I supposed to be the therapist?" She asked. I shrugged my shoulders.

"I may not look smart," I mentally scoffed. "Or act like it. But I've been through enough in my life to know things," I walked back to her and sat down with the bandages in my hand. "I know you and everyone else see me as the young girl who justs trying to make her way in life. And I am. I'm trying to find my way, find where I fit. Find who I am. And I know I've made many mistakes along this ride, but I regret none of them. Because every mistake teaches me a new lesson. That's the difference between you and me. I took my trauma in. I let it get to me and I processed it. I didn't turn my back on it,"

I started wrapping her hand as she looked at me. She's always trying to read me, since the first day I met her. I couldn't help but meet her eyes, and when I did, I felt safe. I felt at home. I felt alive. All these things she makes me feel I couldn't help but wonder if I make her feel the same way. "I liked when you called me Venessa," she whispered.

I looked back down as I finished up her bandages, a smile plastered on my face. "Then Venessa it is," I tucked in the bandage then gave it a slight squeeze. I stood up and walked over to the dresser and grabbed some clothes. The sun was setting and I doubt we'll be leaving the hotel till tomorrow anyway.

"Did you actually...have...feelings for her?" I stopped and stared down at the clothes in my hands with my back facing her. I did have feelings for Veronica. But they were nothing compared to what I felt towards Venessa. Veronica was merely a crush. Venessa was something much more than that.

"I did," silence came and I took that as a sign to leave.

I went into the bathroom and looked into the mirror. I wondered what she was thinking. I always wonder about that. I can never tell and it annoys me. I just want to read her mind, is that too much to ask for?

I started the shower and got undressed.

Once the water hit my body, for a split second, all my problems were gone. I was content and calm. I didn't have a worry in the world. All my focus was on the water touching every inch of my body.

But that calmness left as quick as it came as I felt a cold breeze come across me. "What do you mean, did?" I screamed and covered myself as Venessa swung open the curtains.

"What the fuck!" I yelled as I shivered. I looked up at her to see her eyes roam my naked body. I put my arm across my chest and put my hand between my legs. And as always, she didn't give one shit that I caught her staring at me. "Can I help you?!" I yelled. She finally looked back up at me. And her mood had definitely changed in the last two minutes.

"Did you have sex with her?" I could see the anger rising in her eyes by the second. And if I'm being completely honest. It turned me on more than it scared me.

"What the hell! Get out!" she stepped back from me, in disbelief. Her eyes never left mine. And I guess she must have gotten tired that she couldn't read me. So she started stripping of her clothes.

My eyes became big as she removed her pants and shirt. I turned away, before she could take off anymore, and closed the curtain. As if that's going to do anything.

The cold breeze came again then left. I felt her presence behind me causing my entire to go stiff. I feared that if I moved I would touch her. "Why are you so nervous?" She asked in a very husked tone. Shivers ran down my spin causing my knees to go weak.

My breathing hitched as her front came in contact with my back and she wrapped her arms around me. It wasn't merely the fact that she was naked, in the shower with me. It was the fact that I felt something pressing up against my back. And I knew exactly what it was. "I asked you a question, Miss Wilson," she whispered in my ear. I had to bite my bottom lip from making any noise.

Her lips touched my neck and her hands squeezed my waist. She started slowly planting kisses along my neck, slightly biting every here and there. My mouth quietly gaped open as she ran her tongue from my collar bone to my ear. "Remove your hands," the way her voice flowed through my ear into my body took over me as I lowered my hands.

I could feel her smile against my neck as she moved her hands up my body. Her breasts were pressed into my back as my nipples became hard. "Good girl," she whispered as she took my earlobe between her teeth.

"Venessa," I said in a slight warning tone. She started chuckling in my ear as her hand started to move down my torso.

"Did she touch you?" She asked as her hand grabbed my inner thigh.

"Yes," she hummed in response. She went back to kissing my neck.

"Did she see you naked?" I was too in tune with the pleasure that she was giving me to the point I didn't answer quick enough. She bit down hard on my shoulder making me wince in pain.

"A little," its like anger and frustration just radiated off of her. Her hand slowly inch towards my center as her other hand clenched harder against my waist. Her nails were digging into me, and the bite she left on my shoulder felt like it was throbbing.

"Then I guess that leads to the big kahuna question, now doesn't it?" She stayed silent for a minute. I don't know if she was just trying to soften me up, because she kept kissing my neck, teasing me with her hand, and rubbing my ass. Or if she was just teasing herself. I felt it rising up against my back. I felt the outline of the veins, and they were throbbing. "Did you sleep with her?" She asked me in a tone barley above a whisper, as if she was afraid of the answer.

"No," I could feel her smile from behind me. Both her hands moved away from my waist and onto my shoulders.

"Then I don't see the point of wasting anymore time," she reached forward with her foot and turned off the water. "Now. Final question," she wrapped her arms back around my body and a whimper left my mouth as her cock went in-between my legs, rubbing against my vagina. "May I fuck you Miss Wilson?" My mind went blank as I could only imagine the things that my body was about to go through.

"Yes,"

****

Verbal consent in one of my books? What-What

First Time

Venessa's POV

I couldn't help but smile as I could sense how nervous she was. I wanted her badly, but once I realized what exactly it was that I was doing, I knew I couldn't do what I wanted to right now. She's sensitive. New. A little flower that's just been craving to be touched by someone.

I reached forward with my foot and turned off the water. She silently gasped as the cold air surrounded us. "Now. Final question," I wrapped my arms around her waist, feeling as her breathing became heavy.

My cock had a mind of its own as it slipped between her thighs, slowly running through her folds. I had to stop myself from moaning as I could feel her wetness against me. "May I fuck you, Miss Wilson?" I could feel her body shaking under the presence of mine.

My grip on her waist tightened as I awaited her answer. "Yes," the word slipped off her tongue so easily letting me know that she was finally ready. And I was more than happy to be her first.

A smile formed on my lips as I turned her around. I watched as her eyes looked over the front of my body, and I did the same.

I was breathless as my eyes scanned her. I wanted to touch every inch of her body, slowly. I've never had this much urge built into me and wanted to take it slowly. I wanted to capture this moment. And seeing as this most definitely isn't my first time, I can't even imagine what's going through her mind right now.

But once I looked at her face, her eyes were glued to my dick. I bit my bottom lip as I put my finger under her chin and made her look up at me. I slithered my arm around her waist and pulled her into me. "We're not getting to that tonight, love," I watched as the light in her eyes drained.

"But-" I stopped her with a slow and deep kiss. I don't know why I said that. It came out before I could even understand it. I wanted her, I wanted all of her. But I didn't want to move too fast. My brain was spinning and thinking way too much right now but there was no way in hell I was showing it.

I pulled her bottom lip with my teeth as I moved back.

It wasn't until I heard a moan slip out her mouth that a switch flipped inside of me.

I quickly turned us around and pinned her against the way. A gasp left her mouth as her back hit the cold surface. I immediately reattached our lips but this time with more hunger. I pressed myself up against her as she wrapped her legs and arms around me.

My tongue slipped into her mouth and she put up no fight for dominance. Our tongues circled each other as she ran her hands through my hair. We were both soaking wet but that only made things better.

I pushed off the wall, while holding her ass in my hands, and stepped out of the shower. I walked out the bathroom into the bedroom and laid her down on the bed.

I couldn't tell if her hunger was stronger than mine at this point.

I leaned down on her as she attempted to bring me closer. She started to slowly rock her hips against my torso. I started to kiss down her neck. Lust filled my insides to the point I couldn't even tell the difference. But once I got down to her chest, I started to slow down.

I brought her right nipple between my teeth and softly bit down on it. A soft moan left her mouth as her breathing started to quicken. I licked on her nipple and slowly sucked on it.

Judging by the way her body was reacting to my touch, I have no doubt she would cum any second given the right amount of pressure.

I moved to her other nipple and fondled her breast with my hand. She put her hand on top of my head, trying to ask for me to move down but I wasn't wasting a second with her.

I moved down to her stomach and left little kisses everywhere. I ran my tongue from the bottom of her torso to her bra line. Shivers started to run through her as I left little marks along her body.

I could tell she was ecstasy by the littlest touches I gave her.

I bit down on hip making her flinch but also moan. I left hickeys all along her hips and her inner thighs.

I didn't even touch her center but whenever I looked at it, she was dripping wet. I bit my bottom lip as I could feel myself get harder than I thought was fucking possible.

I lowered myself and looked up to see her staring at me. I gave her a questioning look and she nodded her head.

With a slow motion, I ran my tongue through her slit. She threw her head back in satisfaction and gripped the covers with her hands.

A feeling ran through my body as her wetness sat on my tongue. I could feel the glint in my eyes as I had spread her legs wider.

I moved my hair to the side and kissed her clit.

I ran my tongue through her slit a few more times getting her ready. She started to wiggle out of my view, so I held her down by her thighs with my hand.

It wasn't until I started sucking on her clit that she tried to push me away. I watched as her mouth started to open wide, she wanted to scream but nothing would come out. She put her hand on top of my head as if that could stop me.

I slowly put my tongue inside of her which seemed to push her right over the edge.

I pushed my tongue in and out of her and her grip on the bed sheets tightened. I felt her walls starting to close around my tongue. The only thought that laid in my head was how it would feel having her walls close around my cock.

Her back arched off the bed, a loud scream mixed with a moan, left her mouth. I could see sweat running down her chest and a little on her neck.

I pulled my tongue out and licked up the cum that left her body. She flinched back every once in a while as my tongue touched her sensitive clit.

I kissed her inner thigh, her hip, her abdomen, all the way up her stomach to her breast. I ran my tongue along her neck causing another soft moan to leave her mouth.

I could see she was tired but I wasn't finished. I had too much pent up energy to stop now.

I kissed her chin then finally her lips. Her kisses were sloppy and that's the way I liked them.

While keeping her attention on my lips, I slowly moved my right hand down her stomach in between her legs. I circled her clit a bit and her breathing hitched a bit.

Carefully and slowly, I pushed my middle finger inside of her. Her lips parted from mine as they gaped open. I bit onto her chin as I gave her a second to adjust to my finger.

Once I noticed her body calm down to my touch, I slowly started to move my finger in and out of her. She stayed quiet for a minute or so, trying to get comfortable with the unfamiliar feeling. I tried to make her as comfortable as possible by kissing her neck.

Having the ability to do something that no one else has to someone is liberating. I felt so powerful but for the first time, I wanted to use that power correctly. Anytime I feel this powerful, I abuse and corrupt that power in any way I see fit. But right now, all I wanted was to make her feel good, feel happy. Feel loved.

Once I heard a soft moan leave her mouth I knew to pick up my pace a little. I started moving in and out of her a little faster and her moaning became louder.

I sneaked a second finger in her which slipped in with no problem. I could feel her breathing quicken as her hips rocked against my fingers. I started biting on her ear as her hands went to my back. "You wanna cum?" I asked as I started pumping my fingers a little harder.

She nodded her head while biting her lip, trying to quiet herself. "Well I don't think you should," I whispered as I myself started to rock along with her myself. "I think you should wait. I think you should hold it until I finish," a moan slipped past her mouth sending vibrations down my body. My cock was was getting harder by the second and all I wanted to do was stick myself inside her. "How much do you want to cum?" I whispered again.

Words could form as she threw her head back. I chuckled as I licked my way up her neck. "I need words princess," still, she continued not to say anything. She was on fucking cloud nine right now and I knew there was no way I was getting anything out of her. But I always get what I want one way or another.

"I want you to bed me to cum. Or I stop," I slowed down my pace causing frustration to run through her. A whimper left her mouth and all I did was suck on her neck. "Beg," I growled in her ear.

"Please," she whispered through her teeth. I chuckled and shook my head.

"You can do better than that princess," at this point I completely stopped my fingers and a full blown cry left her mouth.

"Let me cum, let me cum, please let me cum, please, please please," satisfied with my answer I slowly kissed her on the lips and quickly picked back up my pace.

I moved down between her thighs and started sucking on her clit. "Oh fuck!" She screamed as she threw her head back. Her walls tightened around my fingers but that didn't stop me in the slightest. "Aww!" She screamed as an orgasm coursed through her body.

I slowed down my pace, letting her ride it.

I pulled them out and sucked on them while looking down at her.

Her body was covered in sweat, her breathing was haste, and her hair was a mess. I couldn't help but smile as I looked over her. She was worn out.

I leaned down over her and gave her small kisses, whispering sweet little things in her ear.

My breathing hitched a bit as I felt her hand against my cock. I chuckled and shook my head. "Trust me. You're not ready for that princess," she groaned, making me chuckle again.

I got up off the bed and went to grab a rag from the closet. I ran it over water and went back to the room.

She was passed out of the bed and I shook my head with a smile.

I opened her legs and softly wiped her up. She flinched every time I touched her center. I threw the rag in a basket and went to grab some ibuprofen and a glass of water.

I lightly shook her awake and she groaned in the process. "I don't want you waking up in pain, il mio amore " I said in a thick accent.

She slowly opened up her mouth and I rolled my eyes. I placed two of the pills on her tongue and gave her some water. I watched as she swallowed it then laid her head back down. "Good night," I whispered.

I stood up straight and looked down at her. She was so petite. So fragile.

All of a sudden it was like reality hit me. My smile went away, all the feelings that I had experienced in the past hour left. Everything inside me just drained.

No.

Not Ready

I was in pain. So much freaking pain. I barely remember what h appened...I mean I remember. I remember quite fondly actually. But I don't partially remember what happened after.

I woke up today naked covered in a sheet. I was alone in the bed which didn't really surprise me that much. A small ping of disappointment did hit me but I didn't let it flourish into anything more.

I couldn't stop the cringey grin from popping up on to my face. I'm glad no one was around. I felt stupid but I've ever felt better. Although my vagina was was throbbing like fuck, I didn't even mind that much.

Flashbacks of last night kept playing in my head and I didn't dare stop it.

The way she took care of me and focused all her attention on me. I saw a different side of her last night.

I knew today would be different though. I wasn't expecting to wake up to bed in breakfast or anything. I know what type of person she is. It would, though, hurt for her to ignore me. I'm really hoping that doesn't happen but if it does, I will push through today as if last night didn't happen.

I rolled over to the side while slightly groaning. I grabbed a shirt off the ground and slowly stood up and damn near scooted my way out the bedroom.

I didn't hear nor smell anything so I assumed I was probably here by myself. "My vagina hurts," I groaned as I walked into the kitchen. Assuming that I was here by myself was a terrible idea. Because I was indeed, not, by myself.

"Means I did my job," I jumped back as I looked up to see Venessa standing there eating grapes while looking me up and down. I felt my cheeks blush as I looked down at the ground.

"Good morning," I said as I cleared my throat, trying not to sound cheeky. Her eyes followed me all the way to the fridge as I grabbed a water. I had end up bending down, to which I forgot I wasn't wearing underwear. Which I don't understand how I forget that.

When I closed the fridge, Venessa was leaning on the island while staring at my ass. "What?" I said. She raised her right eyebrow then rolled here eyes while chuckling.

"What's with the attitude?" She asked while eating another grape, this time, not looking at me.

I felt bad as I was trying to pretend that nothing happened before she could but ended up hurting her in the process. "I'm sorry. I-I just...well I don't really know what I was trying to do. I guess I-"

"You stutter too much. It's annoying," I stopped talking and looked at her. Now I was annoyed and no doubt my face started to turn red.

She looked over at me and I watched as a smirk appeared. She walked over to me while popping another grape in her mouth. "You thought I was going to act like a bitch this morning so you decided to do it first. I respect that," she walked in front of me, cornering me against the island. She put her hands against the island on both sides of me. "And I actually quite enjoy when you stutter," she leaned into me even more pressing herself against me. A gasp of air left my mouth as she lowered herself to my ear. "It's fucking pathetic," I took a sharp breath in as she leaned closer.

I was prepared for her to kiss me, but instead, she just reached behind me for another fucking grape. I watched as she put it into her mouth and chewed it.

"I want more," I whispered. She lightly chuckled and shook her head.

"Your not ready princess," she said back to me in a soft tone. I must have looked like a child as I started pouting. She bit her bottom lip while looking me up and down with a grin.

"I want. More," she raised her eyebrow as if dating to challenge her.

"I said no,"

"I don't fucking care-" before I could say anything further, she turned me around and pushed my front against the island. She pulled up the shirt I had on and I jumped as her cold hands came in contact with my bare ass. Her finger ran through my slit I had to to suppress my moan. She leaned up against me, I could feel her cock through the sweatpants she was wearing.

"You notice that hesitation in the back of your mind? It means you're not ready. You're not prepared. You can say what you want, but at the end of the day, I am the only fucking person who can give you what you need. So when I say you're not ready. It means you're not fucking ready. Am I clear, Olivia?" The sexual tension building up inside me said one thing but my mouth said another.

"Yes," she slowly got off of me and I turned around to face her with my head down. She put her hand under my chin and made me look up at her. I could see the lust in her eyes but there was restraint. Maybe, she just needed a little push. "What if I show you," I whispered. She squinted her eyes at me. "That I'm ready, that is?" She tilted her head back, in confusion, while biting her lip.

I removed my chin from her hand and without breaking eye contact lowered myself.

It wasn't until when I was completely on my knees that it hit her.

I slowly untied her pants and pulled them down. She kept opening her mouth to stop me or say something but nothing came out. Right when she was finally about to get something out, my tongue touched her tip. I watched as she swiftly closed her eyes and and deeply exhaled. Her dick started to rise up on itself on and I mentally smiled.

*****

You weren't patient, you don't get the rest.

Luv ya

Kidding you guys have been so damn patient with me and I appreciate it very much. Juggling work and school twists my head and body. But I will not quit on this book. I hate when authors quit a story right in the middle of it.

Floor

Venessa's POV

My breathing quickened faster than I care to admit. Seeing her on her knees was a sight that has consumed my dreams many nights, but actually seeing it damn near brought me to mine. I swallowed the lump that was in the back of my throat. Why am I feeling like this? I don't waver. I don't falter. I have brought more women to their knees than I can remember. Maybe it's the fact that I didn't tell her to do so.

As my eyes connected to hers I tried to say something but nothing would come out. What would I say? Stop? There's no way in hell I would tell her to stop. She pulled my cock out of my pants without breaking eye contact with me. I could see she was flabbergasted with it but knew not to show it. She's trying to prove a point, and to do that, you can't show any sort of emotion.

Right when I had decently mustered up what to say, her tongue touched my tip. I closed my eyes and exhaled through my nose. I don't know what switch she flipped on inside me but it was the right one.

I could feel myself getting hard by the second, and not only that, I could feel my senses coming back to me. The wanting, the lust. The power. The feeling I haven't been able to release because this certain someone has been on my mind for so long to the point where I couldn't do what I do best. But now, I have that certain someone in front of me. On her knees. A large grin came to my face and triumph filled me.

Any sort of doubt or questioning I had in me left. Disappeared. As if it was never there. I looked down at her and she knew by the look in my eyes that a whole different person is with her now. I watched as she opened her mouth wider and stuffed my cock down her throat. The feeling of her lips wrapped around me and my tip touching the back of her throat gave me more pleasure than I could even muster.

She slowly pulled back then went back in. I clung to the stove behind me with my hands as she bobbed her head back and forth. I bit my bottom lip as she ran her tongue from my balls to the tip.

My grip against the stove tightened to the point my knuckles started to turn red. My veins were in clear show and my balls were just on the verge of draining. She started sucking on my tip and at that point I felt my toes curl. I pulled her head back by her hair and tightly closed my eyes as I waited for that feeling to go away. I felt her lick my tip again causing me to open my eyes and glare at her.

"What? Don't want to be embarrassed by how fast you cum?" I bit the insides of my cheeks as I started imagining all the things I could do to her little ass.

"I can outlast anyone. Anyday," I watched as a cheeky grin covered her face.

"So, I'm the only person who can make you cum quickly then?"" Out of all the ideas I had, only a certain one lured in the back of my head.

I pulled her hair back tighter making her full neck show. "You wanna be fucked that badly?" She nodded her head. I looked into her eyes, making sure she was in the right state of mind. And when I confirmed that she was. I smiled.

I brought her head back a little bit forward. "Open," was all I said and she obeyed.

I shoved my cock down her throat faster than she could comprehend. Repeadly, I face fucked her until she started slightly choking. And even then, I didn't stop. Watching as her saliva started pouring down her face only made matters better for me. I could feel my orgasm building up again, but this time, I didn't stop.

My tip was continuously touching the back of her throat and she did nothing to fight back. My grip in her hair tightened as I bent over forward and came in her mouth. Not once did she gag or try to pull back. I don't know which was better, my orgasm or the sight of her.

I slowly pulled my cock out of her mouth and looked at her. Her hair was a mess and spit was flowing down her chin."Swallow it" I said coldly. For a split second, she almost listened. For a split second I saw the look I see in everyone else's eyes. Fear. Submission.

But it went away. And she spit it out.

Now, usually....well there is no usually. No one had ever defined me. No one has never not did what I told them to do. So you best believe I felt some type of way when she didn't. Whatever thoughts that were messing with my head I put them aside. Those are private thoughts that no one needs to know I falter with.

So instead I just chuckled and bent down to eye level with her. "Now you get to clean that up," the lust that was in her eyes was on a window view. I watched as she bit her bottom lip and opened her mouth.

"Or what?" I could have punished her. I wanted to. I wanted to fuck the living shit out of her. I wanted to deny her the right to cum. I'm the one who wanted more. And I had the power to do so. Cause I'm the one with the power in her hands. And I always will be. But for the first time in years, my hand wavered.

I put my hands in her hair and forced my lips on hers. She did nothing but moan. My tongue did more than dance with hers and my lips did more than just touch hers.

She rose on top of her knees to where she was hovering over me. I let go of her hair and grabbed on to her waist. She moved to where she was on top of me and not once did we break the kiss. I laid back on the floor and she started grinding on my dick. A moaned escaped my lips.

It wasn't until that sound left my mouth that realization hit me. I have never let someone on top of me. I stopped kissing her and she slowly pulled back, confused. When I looked at her I knew everything was perfect.

And that's what made it wrong.

Why you may ask? Because I don't do feelings. Never have and I never will. That constant feeling of fear of having to worry about someone other than yourself is something I don't take too kindly to.

"What's wrong?" She asked after I didn't say anything. It took me a second to muster up the courage to get from under her. And when I did, I immediately regretted it.

"The funeral is about to start. Go get ready," I walked away before I could turn back around and look at her.

Us

The entire car ride was silent. I would look over at her every so often. Although she looked like she was free of thoughts I knew that was a lie. Either from me or from this funeral, I know she has some type of thoughts running through her head. She's a very composed woman. That's what I love about her. She doesn't show emotion or pain, she holds herself together.

I love that for her. But from experience, I know for her to become like that, something happened to her. That's why I don't really ever pressure her into talking. She'll talk when she wants to. And although whenever she does talk, it may be small things, it's always better than nothing.

I was a little concerned about her right now, but I was also in complete bliss. I lost my virginity. I know that's not something to really celebrate in this era but it was still special to me. Considering I lost it in a way that made me comfortable. By a woman who made me feel wanted.

In spite of the fact that she's kind of ignoring me right now, I'm not taking it personal. I knew she was going to do this.

A smile grew on my face as I started to think. Why am I trying to avoid her so bad? What consequences would come if I do try to pursue whatever this is? Other than me completely getting my heart broken. But hey, what's life without pain.

I guess my smile must have been a little too noticeable because Venessa cleared her throat. I looked over at her while putting my elbow on the window thing and leaned my head against my hand. "What?" I said. She kept glancing over at me.

"Why are you smiling?" I shrugged my shoulders. Does this bitch really got me simping right now?

"Just thinking," was all I said. She came to a stop light and looked over at me. At some point a smile broke out on her face. She looked away and tried to cover it but it was too late. The light turn green and she started back driving.

She only had her right hand on the steering wheel and with the other she was rubbing her face as if to get rid of the tiredness. She had a sleeve tattoo on her right arm. She was wearing a white shirt, to which she rolled up her sleeve to show off her tattoo, and a black blazer over it. She was leaning back in her chair and honestly, I have never been so blown away by the way someone looks as much as I am right now.

"And what exactly are you thinking about?" She asked while keeping her eyes on the road. Again, I shrugged and continued to watch her.

"You I guess," she went silent for a minute. I love how I have come to read her so smoothly in such a short amount of time. She's the therapist and yet here I am. She was trying to act like she didn't care. Like she didn't care what I was thinking. But she wanted to know. "You put up this wall. A very tall and strong wall. And even though you can phase through it, no one can else can even come five feet within it's reach. But the wall is slowly deteriorating. Why that is? I don't know. It may be from me or even from that slutty assistant of yours," she covered her mouth with her hand as she smiled. "Whatever the case may be, you're not happy about it. I mean you are, you're just not used to it. It's like the way your body attacks viruses. It sees something unnatural, and it attacks it. That's why some women loose their first child. Their bodies think its a parasite so it attacks it. And just like the body, when something repeatedly shows up, at some point, you have to just let it in," I watched as she licked her lips.

"So what's the point being made here?" She asked. Her brain was going crazy. She needed an answer. But she wouldn't admit it. I leaned forward to where I was about a foot and a half away from her face.

"I am that parasite. And just like every fucking parasite known to man, I'm going to slip right through that damn wall. I don't care how long it takes, I don't care if I have to disguise myself as something for you won't attack me. But at the end of the day. I will win," finally we came to a stop and she turned off the car. She turned to look at me.

I was serious and I meant every word I said. I'm going to push my way through her. No matter how painful it is. She has made me feel things I never thought I would. And there's no way in hell I'm giving that up.

She leaned into me to where we were less than an inch apart. She grabbed my chin with her fingers and looked down at my lips then back to my eyes. "You right," I small smile played against my lips as I felt her getting closer. I closed my eyes once I could feel her breathing against my skin. "No one comes within five feet of my wall," she let go of my chin and moved away. I sighed and opened my eyes.

She got out the car and closed the door. I sighed deeply and shook it off.

I opened my door and got out then shut it.

I followed her all the way inside the house. There was quiet murmur every here and there. There was definitely a lot more people here now than there was yesterday. Everyone we passed stopped to stare a Venessa. No doubt surprised she even showed up.

I heard a bell ring above my head, signaling the funeral was about to start.

They were burying Venessa's and Veronicas mom in the back of their childhood home. Sweet I guess. More weird it anything. Just knowing that someone is buried in your backyard wouldn't sit to well with me. I guess it would be nice. Then family could go there and talk to her whenever they felt like it.

Everyone gathered in the backyard. I followed Venessa all the way to the back. She had her arms crossed with her sunglasses on. I didn't think it was best to bother her right now, the best I could do was just be there for her. I know she didn't get along with her mother too well but still. Her mom is dead. She has to feel some sort of way.

The ceremony started and it was peaceful. People went up and gave a few speeches. Put followers on the casket.

No tears were being shedded from where I could see. I could only assume that everyone saw this coming and got to spend their last few days with the woman.

I don't feel like going into detail about the funeral because there really isn't anything to tell. I did catch view of Veronica though. She also had sunglasses on, probably covering the black eye Venessa no doubt gave her.

She also seemed non-emotional. And although Venessa did too, at least Veronica looked liked she wanted to be there. Venessa seemed dead inside. The person I got to spend my morning with was gone.

The moment the ceremony ended, Venessa was gone.

I followed her through the house. There was no need to make a statement about my presence because she knew I was there. I followed her all the way up the stairs to the bathroom.

Once we were in, I slowly and quietly closed the door.

She was looking at herself in the mirror as I walked behind her. It was a fairly large room. Especially for a bathroom.

She looked up at me after a while. The look she was giving me made me want to turn around and walk away. But I had my mission. And I was going to stick to it. No matter how long or how hard it was.

Haha, thats dirty.

She sighed deeply out of frustration when she realized I wasn't leaving. "You really want to do this?" She asked. I don't know what exactly she was referring to but I just nodded my head.

She chuckled angrily and snickered.

"Fine," she threw up her hands and turned around. "You think you can fucking handle me?" She started walking towards me. "Then let's find out!" She pushed me up against a wall and slammed her lips on to mine.

The kiss was quick and heavy. I could barely keep up with her, to which I knew was the point.

Her hands went inside my hair as she pulled my head back. Licks turned into kisses and kisses turned into bites as she went all up and down my neck. I could feel the hickeys forming as she started sucking on my soft spot.

A knock came from the door, startling me, but that didn't stop Venessa. If anything, it made her more agressive. The knock kept coming and neither of us made the motion to answer it.

Venessa turned me around and pinned me up against the wall. "Now is not the time for fucking Victoria!" I heard Veronica scream. Venessa didn't give one damn as she started to pull down my pants. But before she could do that, Veronica opened the door.

At that point, I made the motion to stop. Cause no doubt, Venessa would have kept going. "Get. The fuck. Out," Venessa growled.

"Please come back downstairs," Veronica said. Softer than I thought she would. Venessa didn't bother to answer, but instead, started kissing my shoulder.

"You are more than welcome to stay and watch, " she whispered as she started biting my ear. If Veronica wants standing there I would let this woman do whatever the fuck she wanted to do to me.

But there's too much anger. Too much tension. I am a strong believer that you shouldn't have sex without being in the right mindset. Sex doesn't solve issues. Especially relationships issues. Now, I know we're not in a relationship but still. "As..much..as I would love that," I got removed myself from under her and straightened out my clothes. "You two clearly have some things to figure out," I started to walk towards the door.

Venessa grabbed my arm and I turned my head to face her. "If you walk out that door we're done," usually that would hurt someone's feelings. But it made me smile.

"The fact that you admitted there is an us to end, tells me other wise," I winked at her and closed the bathroom door behind me.

Waiting

Venessa's POV

Anger boiled inside of me as she closed the door behind her. But I didn't know where that anger was directed at. The fact that she didn't listen to me, or the fact that she didn't care enough to stay. Nevertheless, I wasn't pleased.

I stared at that door, for who knows how long, hoping and waiting for her to turn around and come back in.

Veronica was watching me.

I don't know if she does this because she's studying me, trying to understand me. Or simply because she just wants to be like me. The way she's looking at me is the look she has given me my entire fucking life.

She's trying to read me, and no matter how hard she tries she will never succeed. It's been nearly over thirty years and she has still yet to know me. "You care about her. Don't you?" She finally said after five minutes of watching me.

I slightly cocked my head and looked at her. She was leaning against the wall with her arms crossed.

I don't feel nothing towards this family, especially her, except disgust. I have come to terms with myself that I am like them though. No matter how much I try and deny it, I am the same broken, fucked up apple that grew on the same dumbass tree as everyone else.

I will never admit that to anyone but still.

"You have put up this wall," I rolled my eyes, "and it has been there for as long as I can fucking remember. I used to think that it was just puberty, hormones, or just a faze. Maybe you wanted to be like everyone else and be mysterious. I gave you your space. Your time. Everything. But whenever those teenage years started to fade off, I rethought my entire childhood. It wasn't any of those things," I was standing across the room as she went to go sit down on the bathtub.

"The day you left home had to be one of the worst nights of my life. I was alone. Finally. I thought I would be happy. I mean, you ignored me my entire life. And whenever you did acknowledge me it wasn't as a sister or even family. But that night I cried myself to sleep. Because after 16 years I had finally realized something. The reason why you acted the way you did was because of me. You hated me so bad to the point you convinced yourself I was invincible. And what's fucked up about all that is the fact that I never did anything to you, except be born. And hell. I wasn't even in control of that,"

I was hearing her. But I'm not sure if I was listening. I've been stubborn my entire life. I know my side of the story. And as far as I know. My side is right. I don't need anyone else's side, I don't need anyone else's viewpoints.

Veronica slightly chuckled as she shook her head. "15," was all she said. We were staring at one another. I wasn't going to comment or ask questions and she knew that. "15 moments," I rose my left eye brow. "That's how many good memories I have of us. Thirty-five years and I only have 15 good memories. Excluding the time you tried to drown me. Terrible at the time but now that I look back at it, I realized you were only just learning to swim yourself," she wiped her forehead with her hand and leaned her head on the wall.

"You have never told anyone your name V. Not even me. I had to fucking go through mamas and babas papers to find your damn birth certificate," I looked away from her and she just sighed. "What I did was dramatic and uncalled for and I apologize. I would say I didn't mean to hurt you but that would be a lie-"

"You tell thought you could use Olivia to hurt me?" I asked. Veronica closed her eyes and slowly shook her head. Disgust filled my insides as I looked at the woman in front of me. But there was a side of me trying to fight it's way out

The side that wanted a sister. Who wanted to hug the woman in front of her and apologize for the decades of pain she caused. The one who was there those 15 moments.

The one who's weak. The one who has been heartbroken one to many times. The one who has no limits of empathy, and in the end, is the one who gets hurt.

"She means nothing to me. No one does," Veronica got off the tub and walked over to me. She was standing in front of me now.

"You told her your-"

"My dick was hard and I needed a release. Nothing new," she squinted her eyes at me.

"Then why haven't you fucked her yet," I slightly smirked and leaned into her.

"You know me sis. The chase is always better than the catch," my words sent shivers down her spine as she took a deep breath in. The amount of fear I can cause this girl always brings a light to me. "And just in case you're wondering. I've already gotten what I wanted," I backed away and looked her up and down. "I know how much you love my leftovers," I winked at her and turned around and walked away.

"That pain in your chest Victoria," I started to open the door. "That feeling you get every time she's around you. When you think of her. When you dream of her. When you imagine what she would feel like wrapped around you. When you think about the way how soft her skin would feel against yours. When you can't even focus on your so called patients anymore," I could sense how close she was to me. "You already know what's happening. You already know how you feel. And you don't need me to tell you. So I'm going to let you slide, V. Because these feelings you have been experiencing are new and terrifying. But if I'm being completely honest with you right now," her breath was against my ear. "I'm just waiting to watch you fall. Watch as everything you built breaks apart. Waiting for you to break apart. And when you do, I'll be right in your corner. Watching, as my big sister who treated me like shit my entire life comes apart. Piece. By piece," she let her words sink into my ear before she stepped in front of me and left.

I felt my insides starting to brun from the inside out. I clenched my hands into fist and bit down on my tongue but nothing worked. A single tear fell.

Because I knew she was right.

******

How do you guys feel about Veronica now?

Want To Be

I am so ready to go.

It's not because of Venessa. Her mind games and bipolarness is actually quite entertaining. Keeps me on my toes. Frustrates me sometimes, but hey, what am I going to do about it?

I'm really just ready to go because I feel that my work here is done. I played Veronica's game, I softened Venessa a little, and I made my goal towards Venessa clear. There really isn't anything for me to do anymore. I served my purpose.

Venessa and Veronica have been in that bathroom for the past fifteen minutes and honestly I'm a little scared. I don't know what Veronica is capable of but I sure as hell know what Venessa is. Or at least I think I do. I still feel like I haven't seen her dark side yet.

The things that I have heard about her make her seem like some psycho bitch. And she probably is. Every once in a while though I go on to her website and look at the comments.

After a while I started reading between the lines and finally saw the meaning behind them. Grant it, about four different people told me what they meant but I just had to figure it out myself.

I was sitting in the back of the room sipping on this wine. I don't really ever drink but my mind was kind of hurting right now. When was the last time she slept with someone? How many people has she slept with? It's not like I would judge her for it but I just want to know. I want to know if she has slept with someone after we met.

I want to know if that assistant of hers still works for her. She probably does but I try not to think about it.

Why does she sleep with her patients? No doubt that's Illegal. Does she do it just for the pleasure of it? Because she's bored? Because she likes using people? These questions with no answers has consumed me for the past month. I thought this process would be over but clearly it's not.

I heard a door close from upstairs, which is highly weird considering I'm downstairs and there's a whole bunch of talking going on and about fifteen different conversations.

Veronica walked down the stairs, still in tact, but looking about disappointed. When her foot hit the last step she forced a smile on her face and joined in a conversation.

I'll give her that.

Veronica hides her problems for the sake of others. She puts on a brave face and pretends like everything's ok, even if it's not. I know whatever happened in that bathroom wasn't perfect but I know both of them got to let out some feelings they've been holding in.

Veronica gave a quick glance around the room until she found me. We stared at one another for a second until she nodded her head at me, as if a sign of respect, and looked away.

Venessa was still no where to be seen so I left my stool from the corner and went back upstairs.

I checked the bathroom to find no one. I looked around upstairs and all the rooms but there was still no sight of her. I swear if this bitch left me.

I sighed as I went into her old room and just looked around. Plane was all I could say. She clearly didn't want to be here by the looks of it.

When I was younger, although I didn't want to be there, I did decorate my room. My room was a home away from home. It was my personal space. It was where I knew I could be by myself. Although my parents were dicks, they never came into my room. Probably because they were to drugged up to even realize I was home.

As I was moving around the room, I stopped and went to go look out the window. Venessa spent a quite amount of time looking out this window. And I knew why.

She had the best view out of the entire house. Your could see the city from a far distance and right behind it were mountains. (A/N. I do not recall what state they are exactly, so let's just assume wherever they are, there are mountains).

But it wasn't until I saw something move out of my peripheral vision that I looked down.

Everyone was inside the house now, except for Venessa.

She was standing over her mother's grave. Looking at it. I couldn't tell if she was saying anything but nevertheless, I could sense she wanted to be alone.

I don't know what I would do if my mother died.

I don't know if I would cry, or be happy. If I would be resentful towards everyone around me or if I would act perfectly normal, as if nothing ever happened. Deep down, I do know I would feel relief of some sort. Solace maybe.

I grew up being hated by the one person who I wanted love from. You don't know what that does to a person. Or at least what that should have done. I should have been a bitch. A person who doesn't believe in love. Someone who only focuses on themselves. In other words. I should have been like Venessa.

But I'm not.

Because I told myself growing up that I would be nothing like my mother. I would be better. I would be grateful and loving. I would give as much love to this world as I could. I would get hurt, and I knew that from the beginning. But I didn't care. Because I wanted to explore.

And for that exact reason is why I'm not giving up on Venessa.

This woman has consumed my mind more than anyone else ever has. She makes me feel things that I've never experienced. She has me smiling every time I hear her name. She has me jealous just knowing that someone else has touched her before. And most importantly, she makes me feel safe and loved. Even when she's being a total bitch, I still knows she cares about me.

I know love is a strong word and I don't think what I feel towards her is that. Or at least not yet. All I know is that I want to be around her. I want to be next to her. I want to be the person she comes to when she wants to talk

I want to be her person.

It was when she looked up towards the sky that I knew it was time for me to go down there. I walked downstairs and out the back doors, making sure no one saw me.

I slowly walked up to her side and stood there silently. I didn't know if she knew I was there but that didn't matter. I heard her sigh deeply as she bent down and put her hand on the tombstone.

"You were right," was all she said. She gave the stone a slightly squeeze and stood up. She looked down at me and I just stood there. There was a little light in her eyes. As if her mind was finally free. As if she was finally free. She slowly grabbed the back of my neck and brought me into her.

She planted a soft and tender kiss on my forehead and sighed once more. "I don't know what to do now," she whispered. I slightly smiled and leaned back out of her grip.

"Me neither. But I do know how parasites work," she rolled her eyes and let go of me. Before she could walk off I grabbed her wrist. She turned back to look at me. "Promise me you'll at least try,"

She looked me up and down. She wanted to say yes but I knew there was no way in hell I would get her to verbally agree.

So instead she wrapped her arm around my waist and pulled me into a kiss. The way her lips felt against mine never ceased to amaze me. "If you can take my dick, then sure," she said against my lips as she pulled back. I started biting my bottom lip.

"If I can take it in my mouth I'm pretty sure I can take it in me," she chuckled in disbelief as she kissed me again, but this one had more tone to it. I moaned in her mouth as her nails started to dig into my waist.

"What, you think just because I fingered you you're not a virgin anymore?" She asked in a husked tone against my ear. I vibration went through my entire body as she started biting on my ear. Thankfully the blinds were closed to the house so no one could see us. "When I'm finished with you princess. The word virgin won't even be in your vocabulary,"

Foreign Feeling

****

The plane ride was tiring and peaceful. Venessa and I didn't talk much but it was a comfortable silence. I smiled to myself in my sleep as the feeling of her embrace embodied me.

I don't remember what I dreamed of but whatever it was, I didn't want to wake up from it.

Her lips would touch my forehead every once in a while, she thought I was asleep but I wasn't. I stayed up most of the time just so I could feel her lips felt against my skin. I'm making her soft. Whether she admits it or not. Grant it, I love the way she is now. And I wouldn't change a thing. She has an authority figure, that I have come to realize, I crave.

I felt arms wrap around my body and all of a sudden I was off the seat. My head rested upon her chest, not once opening my eyes. She carried me all the way into a building that I'd never seen before. We were soon in an elevator and it was quiet.

My eyes were closed but I could feel her chuckling because she knew I was faking it. I felt that if I woke up she would make me walk and I didn't want to.

The elevator soon opened after what felt like forever and she carried me in.

With a slight crack open of my left eye, I could see furniture here and there. I thought we were in another hotel. Which I found weird considering we're back home.

She soon walked into a room where I had to close my eyes completely because if I didn't, I would blow my cover.

She softly laid me down on a bed that was way too comfortable for anyone to sleep on and still get up in the morning. "Pretending is a form of lying. And you know how much I hate that," I snorted with my eyes still closed.

"You have lied to me more than I have lied to you,"

"I have never lied to you," I finally opened my eyes to see her looking down at me. I couldn't help but feel a small ring run throughout my entire body, just because of how she was staring at me. Her hair was pulled back into a bun, looking all professional as always, but she wasn't wearing any makeup, strands of hair flowed past her face freely. She looked like she hasn't been at peace like this in a while.

She's always on alert. She's always dressed to impress, not that she needs to impress anyone, but she never has the time to just relax. Take off her shoes. Be comfortable. I could sense that the moment I met her. But right now, she was content.

Her eyes resembled a forest. Mysterious and beautiful. It has things on the surface that can only be seen with a simple look. But if you go in deeper, you find the poisonous things hidden inside of it. The beauty of the way that poison moves, though, is what will keep you coming back for more.

I felt a rush of energy run through my body as I watched her look away. Her jawline was sharp, just like the rest of her.

I slowly ran my hand up her forearm and she looked back down at me. I motioned with my finger for her to come here and she smirked while leaning down.

Right, when our lips were about to touch she stopped. "You don't tell me what to do, Miss Wilson," I had to close my eyes as her words vibrated through me. She constantly teased me, her lip would touch mine, but only for a quick second, not once kissing me. "I don't care about you," she whispered. I exhaled with a small hum as a response.

"Really," she nodded her head. We were still less than an inch a part from one another. I opened my eyes and so did she. We stared at one another as I put my hand on her left cheek. "Then why are we at your house?"

All the giddiness and cockiness she had in her drained away. I grinned as I ran my hand against her cheek while staring at her lips. "Because if I recall, you said you didn't bring anyone to your house. Now," I started to sit up, feeling confidence run through my veins. "You told me your name, you brought me to your house," I climbed on top of her and straddled her waist. My mouth went next to her ear. "I could only imagine what's next," I slowly took her ear lobe in between my teeth making a small and surprising moan escape her mouth.

Her hands went to my waist, tightening by the second. "You sure you want to do this? Because once I start princess," she looked up at me. "I don't stop,"

I slowly moved my ass against her hip giving her all the temptation she needed. "Do your worst. Dr. Morgan." Her hands started to go into my shirt, undoing my bra.

"Safeword," I rose my left eyebrow, "pick one," within a swift motion, my back was on the bed and she was on top of me. "Today Miss Wilson," she damn near growled at me as she took off her shirt.

"Light," she didn't question it one bit and instead attacked my neck with her mouth. A moan escaped my mouth before I could stop it and my arms wrapped around her body. I could feel how eager and hungry she was just by the way her body moved against mine. I was scared when Veronica approached me because I feared how rough she would be. I have no doubt in the back of my mind how rough Venessa is about to be, and I have never wanted something so much in my life.

Her tongue moved around in circles against the crook of my neck as she started to leave marks. She planted her teeth in my skin, and although it hurt, the pleasure overruled that pain.

This bitch literally ripped off m shirt and tore off my bra. My back arched into her once I felt her mouth wrap around my nipple. The way her tongue felt against my chest had my body in Euphoria. My head was on cloud nine and I never wanted it to stop. She traced her tongue all the way down my stomach, stopping every once in a while to leave a mark.

Once her lips reached my abdomen I put my hands on top of her. Gently I feel that I have to add. Because the way she gripped my wrist and glared at me you would think I was the one who forced my dick into her mouth less than a week ago. She rose up and hovered over my body with hers. "I'm too horny to explain my rules to you but one major one. Is that you don't touch me unless I tell you to. Am I clear?"

My sensitive ass would have backed into a corner by now, but the thing is. I'm in control here.

I'm the one who gets to give her her release. I'm the one who tells her to stop and when to go.

I ran my finger from her lower abdomen all the way up to her chin. Making sure my nail was leaving a trail. "You've been doing a lot of things with me that you don't do with anyone else," her glare never stopped and neither did the lust in her eyes. I slightly smirked as I rose and put my lips next to her ear. "So why stop now?"

With a swift of a finger, I flipped us over to where I was on top of her. Surprise felt her face but I stopped her before she could do anything about it. She started to get up but I held up my finger. "You get up, I stop," for a split second there, adoration felt her eyes. That look in your eyes that you get when you see a mountain for the first time. Or a beautiful waterfall in the middle of the forest. That look went away though once she noticed I was watching her.

"It's cute honestly," she said. I cocked my head to the side in questioning. "It's cute that you think you have any control. How you think after all this time of knowing you, and I haven't stuck my dick inside you, you strongly believe I'm going to allow you to take over," she started shaking her head while grinning.

She slowly sat up while tightly gripping my waist. "I'm not letting some inexperienced virgin be in control of me. Especially not when she's been fucking teasing me for so damn long," She flipped us back over and took off my pants. "But you're in such a hurry, I will gladly obey,"

She didn't give me any time to prepare as she slid her tongue through my slit. A feeling that I have still yet put a name to, ran through my body. My hands grabbed a fist full of the sheets as her tongue circled my clit. Moans left my body quicker than I could catch them. My thighs, out of instinct, attempted to close themselves, but she held them apart. I could feel her nails digging into my thighs as she started sucking on my clit

"Fuck," I whispered as I could feel my orgasm building by the second.

A groan came through once the feeling slowly left my body. Before I could complain about her teasing me, a mixture between a moan and a scream left my though. A small moan left her mouth too as her cock throbbed inside of me. She laid down on top of me as both of us adjusted to the foreign feeling. "If I would have known you felt this good Miss Wilson, I would have fucked you that day in the school bathroom," the way her words flowed through my body was something I will never get tired of.

CPSIA information can be obtained
at www.ICGtesting.com
Printed in the USA
LVHW030556020223
738427LV00015B/1292

9 781805 092360